THE LIGHT PEOPLE

THE LIGHT PEOPLE

A Novel

By
Gordon Henry, Jr.

Michigan State University Press
East Lansing

"The Prisoner of Haiku," "Haikus and Dream Songs of Elijah Cold Crow," and "Bombarto Rose: A Note to Hold the Eyes" were previously published in *Earth Song, Sky Spirit*, ed. Clifford E. Trafzer (New York, N.Y.: Doubleday Books, 1993)

Michigan State University Press
East Lansing, Michigan 48823-5245

Printed and bound in the United States of America.

09 08 07 06 05 04 03   1 2 3 4 5 6 7 8 9 10

LIBRARY OF CONGRESS CATALOGING-IN-PUBLICATION DATA
Henry, Gordon
The light people : a novel / by Gordon Henry, Jr.
p. cm.
ISBN 0-87013-664-X (alk. Paper)
1. Indians of North America—Fiction. 2. Minnesota—Fiction.
PS3558.E4974 L5 2003
813/.54 21

Cover design by Heather Truelove Aiston.

Cover art is *untitled*, 26 May 2002, 12" × 15", prisma color pencil on paper by Star Wallowing Bull. Photo is used courtesy of Bockley Gallery, Minneapolis, Minn.

Visit Michigan State University Press on the World Wide Web at:
www.msupress.msu.edu

Dedicated to Southern Spirit Woman, Young Thunder Woman, Rainbow, Little Star, White Cloud Woman, Old Eagle (the elder), Eagleheart, and Old Eagle Woman.

CONTENTS

ACKNOWLEDGMENTS

I am most grateful to Professors Bob Lewis, Jay Meek, Michael Beard, Bill Borden, and James Vivian for their encouragement and for their honest commentary on early drafts of this manuscript. I would also like to thank Professor Lewis for his patience with me and my years of serious investigation of procrastination methodology. (I wish him the best in his residence on the Turtle.) Likewise, Jay Meek, Bill Borden, and Michael Beard deserve special thanks for helping me improve my writing skills and for inspiring me with their imaginative work and insights.

Many more thanks to the people in the UND English Department and to the faculty and staff in the American Indian Studies Department at UND. I would also like to acknowledge all those North Dakota people who taught and strengthened me with their words and deeds; they include Francis and Rose Cree, Louis and Liza Cree, Jessie, Debbie, Erin, and Greg Cree, Jim McKinzie, John Salter, Joe Deflyer, Richard LaFramboise, Jake Thompson, Theresa (Henry) Thompson, and all the thirsty dancers.

I am also grateful to George Cornell, Diane Wakoski, Phillip McGuire, and Sheila Roberts, who encouraged me to continue while I was at Michigan State University.

Thanks to my friends and colleagues at Ferris State University, particularly John Alexander, for pressing for free time for me and for supporting the development of American Indian courses at Ferris. Big thanks to John and Roxanne Cullen, Richard Branson, and Phillip Middleton for their enlivening friendship, for their supportive spirit, and for their weak humor during my tenure at Ferris.

To the people at the University of Oklahoma Press, Kim Wiar, Sarah Nestor, Larry Hamberlin, Patsy Willcox, and Cathy Imboden, I am grateful for the guidance and professional expertise they provided in bringing this work to publication.

Many thanks to Gerald Vizenor for the fine work he has done over the years in support of American Indian literature. I am also grateful to him for encouraging me to publish this novel.

My thanks to the storytellers, the rememberers, and the remembered: Francis Cree, Louis Cree, Bill Henry, Jr., Marie Fairbanks, Irene Vizenor, Joseph Vizenor, Jr. (Sonny), Mox Vizenor, Angie and George Ross, Rena, Toni, and Cleo.

Heartfelt thanks to those Native people whose work has inspired me. Thanks to Carroll Arnett, Joseph Bruchac, Lance Henson, Patrick LeBeau, N. Scott Momaday, Gerald Vizenor, James Welch, Leslie Marmon Silko, Linda Hogan, Louise Erdrich, Winona LaDuke, George Cornell, Dale Hanks, Gordon D. Henry, Sr., and Wilma Henry.

THE LIGHT PEOPLE

INVISIBLE TRAILS

As a child under blinking constellations, in the conversations of old people, he imagined a man descended from the sky, streaming arrays of star life into the deep reflective ocular fires he sometimes saw in the face of his mother, Mary Squandum, as she stroked his hair or shifted his collar. Or he thought of the man as a fierce wind who cast stones upon the living world and through the force of wind blew the stones whole into the bodies of living beings, or who blew so hard, so wildly that he worked the stones on the exterior, sculpting the living form, while leaving the interior life to itself. At other times, in the space of a moon-struck room, he saw the man across from him, dimly lit, at the edges of a fire between sleeping and waking. Then at some point his father became unnameable, unreachable, the introspective absence of a conclusion, an alloted X of an intellect tangled in a village of stories and imaginative encounters. In the village some people told him his father was a Pillager, a descendant of Lightning; some people called him a Stone; some said he was Pembina, a Basswood. One old woman told him his father left the village alone, with another boy, during an outbreak of trachoma. Some people in Four Bears Village didn't know him. Oskinaway never saw the man outside of the workings of his own head. He came to no final conclusion.

His mother vanished on the powwow trail. He awoke one morning to geese crossing the spring sky in the frame of the window in the back room of his grandparents' peeling red house on the reservation. He heard honking and ran out front to catch a glimpse of his mother climbing into the back of a lustrous blue van with a panel of mountain scenery painted on the side. His mother carried her powwow regalia on a hanger, wrapped in plastic, in one hand; in the other she held the handle of a suitcase and the pheasant fan she danced with. He called out, but sliding metal doors and the sound of an engine came between his words and their destination.

The man in the van was a trader, a bookseller, a purveyor of supposedly mystical weavings and other metaphysical hangings, which were marketed as Native-produced spiritual crafts. Reservation people said the man called himself Rainbow, but he had many names. Some knew him as Arthur, some as Stone Bull, some as Dude, some as Jackson. Oskinaway didn't care what his name was. He watched his mother leave and he waited for her return. He went to powwows on the hands of old ones and thought he would find her there and take her hand. He believed he saw her a few times: once, at the June 21 celebration, she was whirling around in the dance circle, shawl-dancing, stepping among hundreds of revolving dancers, waving her fan in short strokes, sometimes high, sometimes low before her face; he joined in, dancing toward her, but when he reached the woman, he didn't recognize the face and he walked out of the circle, all the way home. On another occasion, at his auntie's house in South Minneapolis, he saw a powwow on public television, and when the camera came in for a close-up he was sure he saw her. He cried out, "Come quick, it's her," but by the time his cousins came, by the time the family had gathered around, the camera had pulled back and refocused on the black- and yellow-beaded designs of thunderclouds on the moccasins of another dancer's feet.

On the day his mother ran away, he ran toward the river, toward a particular silence that is moment to moment, measured by the distance between the whistling anger of redwing blackbirds, the calls of crows, and the sounds of his own human footsteps too close to hidden animal spaces. But those sounds faded too when he reached the river and peered in. Everything rushed past then, the sky, the earth beneath the layer of reflecting brown skin, green and yellow leaves, broken limbs of dead trees, dragonflies and skimmers, a fisher sluicing water as it made its way into a village of reeds. Then he reached into the water to pick up a flat smooth stone, the only thing he could see that did not move in the river's flow, and as he put his hand into the water he felt the strength of the river pull at him, holding him to the river. At first he tried to pull back, but the river had him, and he did not have the strength to remove his hand. So he let the river hold him and he studied his face, the river, his river face punctured by his wrist, his hand beneath the face. Everything rushed past; clouds flowed away, volume after volume of white mist, turned to still, red, sundown wisps. Then when the same sundown red drew down upon the face of the river he heard movement in the brush on the opposite bank. A boy came out of sundown shadow, laughing, stood by the edge of the water, laughing. He laughed for a long time as he looked at Oskinaway with his hand in the water.

Finally he said, "you won't catch anything that

way. That's not a good way to catch anything. Pull
your hand out of there."

Oskinaway called back, "I'm stuck, the river's got
me," and when he said this he looked down and his
face was gone in the darkness, and he pulled again to
test the river. When he came free he heard the laughter again, and he looked out across the river, but the
other boy was gone.

So he remained with the old ones, his grandparents, and he was raised according to their varied
ways and beliefs. He went to the mission school,
where he learned history, the manipulations of numbers, to read and write. He started on the same path
every morning, from the two-track outside his grandfather's door, on down the dirt road, along Sucker
Creek, past the Episcopal church, to where the road
came into a Y, where the main road from Four Bears
village ran into the road of his relatives, where the
schoolyard spread out from the mouth of the Y.
Among school teachers he was known for his
reserve; among schoolchildren for his solitude,
his speed afoot, and his ability to throw balls with
a velocity beyond the power of the older boys. He
shot high arcing jump shots with an unstoppable
accuracy throughout those same boyhood years.

On school year afternoons, during the extended
days of summer, through changes in seasons, his
family prepared him for different lessons. From his
grandparents he learned plants, medicines, the seasons' movements, and changes in animal behavior
and sources of survival. He learned of different
beliefs: the old ones took him to church on Sundays
and sent him to his room when the jessakid jugglers
and sucking doctors came to the house late at night to

divine truths and render healings to people in the village. In time, he knew what went on. He slipped out
from his room and crouched in the corner, watching.
Through a doorway, he saw the man called Jake Seed
working in low light, smoke rising around him,
the smell of cedar and tobacco in the air. A bowl of
water shimmered at the old man's side, the sick one
stretched out on a blanket on the floor. The old man
sang into the dim room through the night, the room
whirled on his voice, shifting in depth and intensity
of light. Then Seed pulled out a bone tube and drew
in his breath, specks of luminous breath, deep sigh-
ing breath, and he lifted his head quickly and spit
dark, shiny liquid and clumps of tissue into the
wooden bowl. Then he called a member of the sick
man's family up to his side, and while the relative
waited he covered the sickness with cloth.

"Tomorrow you must bury this," he said. "Find
a place of sunlight, where it shines down onto the
earth, beside a white pine. Bury the cloth there with
a tobacco offering."

As he grew, Oskinaway questioned the old people
about diviners and healers, and they answered each
time with long stories about the nature of gifts and
human responsibilities. As these stories passed, he
felt the village past rising up on a great road, walking
toward him in his dreams, pointing to the earth and
sky as it approached. But the past never reached him,
the road ran into sundown seasonal apparitions, and
one summer during a storm Oskinaway grew scared
and he cried late into the night until the storm subsided. At the table the next morning he asked his
grandparents to call someone to find his mother.

Four days later his grandparents took him to Jake

Seed's place with the boy's request. Seed's house
set deep in the woods beyond the best of the reservation gravel roads. There a two-track ran through a
weeded center and sand and mud wheel ruts to the
bush behind Rush Lake, not far from the old grave
house remains. The house peeled black tarpaper. A
silver stovepipe puffed thin blue woodsmoke out,
just off to the side of the apex angle of the roof. When
the family pulled up, in a coughing red Galaxy, four
dogs stood up from various points near the small flat
front porch and ambled around, circling and back-
tracking in their own continuous barking. Seed
showed the three people in and offered each a chair
at the kitchen table. As the boy sat down he looked
around the room, gazing momentarily at items inside
the tight kitchen and through the narrow doorway,
which leaned to the right, away from the village side
of the house. In those gazes the boy saw the uneven
floor beneath his feet, rising up in small humps and a
few barren spots worn through beneath the faded
pale yellow of dull floral prints. Through the doorway Oskinaway saw Seeds of the past, resting in
black-and-white photos on the wall, enshrined in
human articles of remembrance, like a bronze statue
of a boxer, fighting a sun band, posed for a nonexis-
tent opponent, beneath a window showing a glimpse
of two-track, bending away into trees. Beyond the
photographs, toward the center of the room, partly
severed in an incomplete view by the door frame, the
young man saw a mirror, reflecting part of the other
wall and the tin pipe of a wood stove. An engraved
copper medallion hung over the top right-hand corner of the mirror. As the boy contemplated the face of

the ornament, Seed brought coffee and sugar and a can of evaporated milk to Oskinaway's grandparents. As they drank, Oskinaway's grandfather came to the purpose of the visit.

"This boy," he said, nodding to Oskinaway, "wants to know about his mother. She's been gone for a while now. He saw her run off with a trader when he was about seven years old. We all thought she would return in a few days or weeks, but it's been a few years and we haven't seen her since. A few of our people down in the cities say they've seen her here and there, but by the time we catch word of such things, it's too late. Sometimes he cries about her. He asked us to find someone who could help find her. He also wonders about his father. We tell him some things, like when and where he was born, but his mother never made anything certain, even to us."

With that the old man reached into his right breast pocket and pulled out a can of tobacco. He offered the can to Seed. Seed studied the boy and gestured to the old man to give the tobacco to Oskinaway. Oskinaway took the tobacco and offered it to Seed himself.

Seed accepted the can. "You know what can be done, Jim. Sometimes memory runs away from us and even the spirit can't find the trail. In some cases people leave things in a particular place and wander further and further away from that place with the false knowledge that what they left will always be there. Sometimes, then, the lost must want to return, before their knowledge makes them forget what they left. Still, I go by what I am given. I never know how these things will turn out. Sometimes the people who come to me already know the answer. Sometimes they don't know what they really want."

Seed paused then as he opened the can and rolled a cigarette. He raised the cigarette up and pointed in four directions around the room. After he lit the cigarette he spoke again. Smoke rolled out with his words, turning and gesturing in speech into invisible conclusions in sun bands behind the old man's head. Then Seed turned to the boy. "In a few days I'll send a young man to see you. He'll tell you the meaning of certain things, of things I believe in. He is strange, but he is a helper and he will tell you the meaning of magic as he understands it. He will also tell you when to return for the ceremony to find your mother."

Two days later the old ones prepared for Seed's messenger. Grandmother put out corn soup, fry bread, wild rice, boiled potatoes, rabbit, and rhubarb pie. The old man gathered and prepared red-willow tobacco and wintergreen and brought down some smudging and dried mint from the wall. Oskinaway met Seed's helper at the screen door.

"Boozhoooooooo," the man said as the boy opened the door. He was a young man, different in inflections and mannerisms. He carried himself differently, with a dissonance of gestures gathered in faraway places and circumstances outside the reservation. He spoke with different intonations. He wore a white baseball cap with silver and red beadwork around the front rim of the bill of the cap. Two braids of dark brown hair, wrapped in red cloth, hung down from the sides of his cap behind his ears. The rest of his clothes were mostly black. He wore a black suitcoat with a white eagle appliqué on the back. A red-beaded woodland flower design rose from the left breast pocket of the coat in an intricate green-leafed vine that stopped with the red blossom near his shoulder. Underneath the coat a silver woodland landscape opened between the lapels against the black background of a T-shirt. Under the landscape, again in silver letters, in a two-line slogan, the shirt read, "Save a tree / tell a story." His pants were black denim, worn at the knees, and he wore black pointed western boots with red thread in the design. When he came into the kitchen, the old woman set the table and they all ate together. Throughout the meal few words passed between the old people, Oskinaway, and the messenger from Seed.

After dinner the old people led Seed's helper to another room. There they settled into comfortable positions: Oskinaway sat on the sofa covered with an old green blanket. Seed's helper settled beside him. The old man sank back into his favorite blue chair near the wood stove while the old woman went to the dresser against the long wall of the room to gather materials for a weaving, before she sat down in a rocker not far from her husband. Then the old man rolled two red-willow cigarettes. When he finished he nodded to Oskinaway and the boy walked over, took one cigarette, and gave it to the messenger. The men relaxed there in silence, smoking, following the smoke with light-specked eyes as evening spread out, down and around the house and the village, in engulfing darkness the attendant echoes of sundown dogs, thick volumes of crickets, and in their pauses, nighthawks and wind vibrations singing through the structures of the house. When the last sparks of the cigarettes flared away, Oskinaway felt sleep growing in him, filling him with measured rhythms of tiredness that he fought and controlled only for a time as Seed's messenger began to speak.

ARTHUR BOOZHOO ON THE NATURE OF MAGIC

I'm different, you may have noticed. I was raised far away in a city. My father went there under relocation to work for a utility company, electrical people. After a few years he died; he was falling, they say, and to save himself he reached up and grabbed at some wires and was electrocuted on the spot. I was ten. We moved around quite a bit after that. We lived with my aunties and uncles, but there were so many of us we caused hardship, so we didn't stay in one place long. About four years later, my mother met a man somewhere when she was out drinking with her sisters. They married, but the man didn't want anything to do with us, so they sent all the kids away to live with our grandparents. By then I was seventeen, and I made up my mind to stay in the city.

While my brothers and sisters returned to the rez, I got work part-time in a candy factory, and I was doing pretty good for a while. In a few months I bought a car and I could drive all over. I drove to see my mother once at a place in San Francisco, but the visit didn't seem to mean much to her so I left. After a year or so I got letters from my grandparents here asking me to come back, but I had already decided to go to college part-time. After I wrote back to tell them about my plans, they wrote and told me I could go to school full-time with tribal funding, at a school closer to the reservation. Instead I applied and got financial aid to attend college at San Jose State the next fall. At first I wanted to study everything, but after two or three terms, a counselor told me I should consider one field. I chose drama. I felt I could act, and that if I chose many different roles maybe I'd find the one I was closest to and live it. While I was taking the drama course work, I got involved with a group of people who believed that everyone has a personal magic that they can ignore or use. We'd all meet once a week to discuss those mystical concepts and study magic. By the end of the year all but two people had dropped out of the group. So there was just me and one woman. At our last meeting she told me the only reason she stayed in the group was because she loved me. I didn't know what she meant, and I told her I thought she was a very magical person, but I didn't think I loved her. That was the last I saw of her.

But I was in love with magic. So I quit school and I went around the city seeking out magicians and gathering an assortment of tricks and teachings from each one. I also studied magic books, every one I could find. In time I knew enough to make a living from magic, with illusion and memory tricks. But I wasn't sure about things. I kept getting letters from my grandparents and my brothers and sisters. They all wanted me to return to this place, the place of my grandparents, my ancestors. One letter brought me back. My youngest sister was sick. Doctors found no cure, and she was next to death. I got in my car and drove for two days straight.

When I got to my grandparents' house they took me into the room where the girl was dying. The light was such that her head was a shadow growing up from the bed with the floral print of the sheets.

I spoke to her: "Do you know who I am? Can you see me?"

The shadow turned from the window and became
a face. I knew then her eyes didn't register. I was
unrecognizable, so I moved closer. Grandmother
tried to pull me back.

"It's catching, trachoma," she said. "Young people
all over the reservation are dying."

But the child's voice moved me forward to the edge
of the bed.

"Do you know magic?" she said. "Show me some
magic, brother."

"Can you see me?" I said.

"No," she said, "I can't see you, but I remember
seeing you."

"Then I can't do magic."

My sister turned her head to the window; sunlight
surged out over her face, soaking into her skin, light-
ing her clearly, as I now see her in my mind.

"I can only see light," she said.

Two days later she died. In a week I came onto the
same sickness. I could feel my sight going, but it was
like the going had nothing to do with what I saw or
what lived outside me. My sight was going from the
inside, almost backward, like the memory of the
operation of the eyes left out particulars and details,
like my head was shoveling the inner light I needed
to see into a great mound of expanding and hungry
shadows.

I asked my grandfather about magic. "We have
none here," he said, "at least not the kind you know,
of the hand and the eye and memory games. But
there are healers among us, men and women of gifts
and visions. Some are relatives of light people. Sometimes their gifts can bring people back. Quite a few
people have told us not to believe in those gifts, but

with all the sickness around us and no cures by the
white doctors, some people have returned to these
descendants of the original teachers and bringers
of light."

Then the old man took me to Jake Seed and he
healed me. When I was well I went to Seed again and
asked if he could teach me the magic he had. He told
me to come every day and he would decide if he
could teach me. I went to his place every day for
about four years. Then he put me through a ceremony. After days of preparation and explanation of
the meaning of the ceremony, he took me way back
into the woods behind his place. We walked up a hill.
I dug a hole; he prayed over it and put tobacco down.
I stepped down into the hole and waited. Once again
he prayed. Then he put a ring of tobacco around me
and buried me up to my neck.

*Darkness swelled out of the earth swallowing shadows,
leaving only the light of animal's eyes and distant stars to
compose the sights I saw. I was not there long when animals
came shining low to the ground. They moved up to my face,
scratching the earth, scratching dirt into my eyes. After a
while, minutes, hours, a thousand blue blinks of stars, a
hundred rustlings in the trees, animals sat in a circle
around me, outside the ring of tobacco, growling and moan-
ing. Then I understood their language and I felt fear for all
of creation. My thoughts raced in the darkness to find the
old man, but my body was still in the hole, nervous, shivering in the cold night dirt. There was no magic to match the
feeling; no illusions could pull me from the ground. I waited
for power and I sang like I always do when I'm nervous. The
first song came out rough, a coarse melody, bent with fear,
like a sapling resisting strong wind. The deeper I went into*

the song the more I felt the fear slacken into a strength of human sound mixing with air and elements. Soon the animals joined in, growling to long musical howls, introspective calls and silences. My own vocals hung on for a long time; note faded into note; song faded into song. There were words and there were no words; there were sounds and there were voices from the once fearful gut, grasping each musical moment. Then, when the songs grew longer, I knew no more of the source of the memorized and invented tones. The animals left. I felt their shadows slink back out of the circle and bolt away, skittering across dirt into the leaves, into the bush. In silence and solitude, I heard footsteps behind me; then laughter careened, in a strange dance. I finally caught sight, out of the corner of my eye, of a small person. At first, I thought he was a child, but as he drew closer I knew he was a little man. He had a small drum in his hand and he sang in laughter.

Red day coming
Red boy dreams
Red day coming
over the back of clouds

Eye of the Eagle
Swift and Swallow
Red day coming Red boy sings

Then the little man stopped, turned his back to me, and he wheeled back around. He held his enormous penis in his hands and pissed on the ground in front of me, close enough that I could see steam rising from the earth and smell and feel the sprinkle of his spray as he snickered. When he finished he abused me with gruff, untranslatable language, and he kicked dirt into my face. He swung his drumstick and struck the back of my neck with a force that astonished me with pain and the little man's power. I felt the sting of the blow vibrate in violent waves down to my feet. I rocked and twisted in the hole. I screamed, wailing anger. I cried, "Go away." I called to the spirit of god for mercy. But the little man stayed. He clubbed my ears, he crapped in front of me and danced with joy at my pain and degradation. Then I gave up. "Go ahead," I said, "do what you want, I surrender." Right then, in the middle of a wild raucous dance, in the middle of his ridiculing laughter, he stopped and sang again, a song of sorrow.

sees the fading stars
sees the northern lights
sees the eyes of animals
all in the face
all in the face

the face eats
the face speaks
boy and man
the faces love

the faces love the stars
the faces love the ghost lights
the animal faces
the faces eat
the boy and man
speak and eat
the faces they love

With that the man trudged off toward a huge stone, and walked around and vanished behind it. There the sky was

coming onto dawn, and light shone red over and through
the eastern trees.

Seed came up then, carrying a basket and a piece of
red material. He sat down on the ground a short distance in front of me, took out a tobacco pouch and
rolled up a smoke. For a long time he said nothing.
Then he got up, reached into his basket, and brought
out a plate of food. I smelled the boiled potatoes, and
my eyes rested on the boiled meat as he set the plate
in front of me. Next to the plate he set down a glass
of water. "Let the eyes drink for you. Let the eyes eat
for you," he said. Then he picked up the plate and
ate the food, bit by bit, in slow reflective mouthfuls.
Once in a while he took a sip of water. Throughout
the meal he never said a word. When he finished the
meal, he took the red material and twisted a handful
of tobacco up inside it. Then he tied the material to
a tree, toward the east, about fifty feet away from
where I was buried.

That day the sun burned the memory of thirst and
hunger into me. I grew angry at the sun, at Seed, at
myself. I tried to sing again but my throat didn't work
in the heat, in dryness. Then I cried. I cried for the
rest of the day until the sun went down. At night I
tried to sleep, but the animals returned, encircling me
and keeping me awake. Just before dawn I heard
laughter. I thought of the little man again, but I
couldn't see anyone or anything in any direction. At
last the sun pushed out red light, and I saw out in the
east, on the tree where the tobacco was tied, a woodpecker, one of those big ones, pileated. The bird was
laughing, driving its beak into the tree in the dawn

light. Light streamed out from each place the woodpecker struck, as if the tree held its own sun inside and the bird conducted the light of that sun out. Time and again the bird backed off, lifted away from the tree, and landed on another part of the tree to peck and strike another place from which light flowed out. One final time the bird did this. Then the bird reached into the tree with its beak and extracted the light in a long bending waving string that followed the course of its flight to where it circled me. Then the woodpecker flew down over the hill out of my sight, with the long string of golden light trailing behind it. From there I saw Seed approaching, and after he dug me out I left the hole and the hill.

By the next spring it was clear that Seed had accepted me as his helper. Through him I learned to assist with ceremonials. At the same time, I continued practicing the magic I learned in the city, among the people of the reservation and the people of nearby communities. I ran ads in local news publications, and I posted my card on bulletin boards outside grocery stores, outside the tribal offices, all over. I got a few jobs but the work wasn't steady, so I started working part-time as a janitor at the Original Man School.

Things were going well for me. I was learning and I had work; I was surviving. Then in the fall I did my magic act for a children's birthday party in a town outside the reservation, in Detroit Lakes. I performed my most difficult tricks with the most success I'd ever had. One was a mentalist memory trick through which I heard, and recited back with my eyes closed, the names and details of clothing of every person at the party. For the other most difficult trick I had the

birthday child rip up a piece of his parent's most
important correspondence and put the ripped pieces
into a fishbowl full of water. Then I threw my magic
coat over the bowl and sang.

Sleep, peels, angles of angels sing of sign,
sword of words, elm smells concrete, encore
on the corner, a northern ornithologist, jest
in case, sends a letter which ends in ways to
sway opinion to slice the union onion with a
sword of words, without tears.

After that and the conventional magical smoke,
the child retrieved the letter from the family mailbox
and returned to show everyone that the ripped-up
correspondence was whole and dry. Everyone was
impressed; I was impressed; the children were
impressed; the parents were impressed.

When I returned to the reservation to see Seed, to
tell him about my success, a young woman met me at
his door. She told me that she was Seed's daughter,
Rose Meskwaa Geeshik, that the old man was sick.
She had come to see him after a violent disturbing
dream and found him sweating, fevered and weak.
"He's been reciting names," she said. "Oskinaway,
Minogeshig, Broken Tooth, Kubbemubbe, Shago-
nawshee, Bwanequay, Nawawzhee, Yellowhead,
Abetung, Aishkonance—he repeats the names and
shivers. I don't know what it means."

In the time I worked with Seed he never mentioned
any living family or any children. She took me back to
see the old man. I followed her to the back bedroom.
Seed slept there, on the bed, wrapped in a star blanket. Sundown named the hour in the window of the

room. The songs of faraway crows coruscated into
the room in sundown angles. I spoke to him. "Seed,"
I said, "it's me, Boozhoo. How are you? Seed, wake
up; I need to speak to you." For a long time there was
no answer. Darkness worked into the room and only
an occasional cigarette, the flare of a match, touched
off any semblance of sight. After a time Rose asked
me to pray with her for Seed. She called on grand-
fathers, the creator; she spoke of her love for the old
man. Her eyes squeezed tight in the intensity of her
thought.

Creator bring him back to us
he is far away now within the sight of
    ancestors
their arms are open across the silver river
there are giants and abysmal sorrows in the
    river
Some of us will float over
Some of us will find the water solid beneath
    our feet
Some will step on the backs of the giants
    and slide away
into an angry foam
Some will sink straight down into a place
where the river has no bottom.

O creator do not take the man
Dear ancestors sing a song that tells it is not
    time
turn him back to us with your song
Let Seed return to earth
Let the skies drench him again

Let him know again the fragrances of the
    great mother earth
Let him draw his strength from the love
    that is here
in my heart.

Rose prayed on and on, crying off and on between
the words, at times screaming out into the darkness
of the room, with a voice and a hope powerful
enough to wake the most distant sleeping star. Still
Seed didn't move; his face showed no change. Rose
prayed on and on. I wanted to stay awake to help
her, but only fear ever kept me from sleeping and at
that time I felt no fear: maybe it was Rose's voice,
maybe it was the strength I'd seen in Seed in times
past, but I felt no fear.

*Somehow I have come to sit on a log. After thinking I am
asleep, I understand I am awake when a yellow dog crosses
in front of me. Voices inside the log tell me I must learn to
fly. So I make a man out of tall grass and call him by my
own name. Then I throw him into the air and a whirlwind
of leaves and human voices carries the grass man away.*

Rose woke me at dawn with a gentle hand on my
shoulder. "Have some coffee," she said, offering me
a yellow cup. "He'll be okay, now."
I took the coffee cup from her. "Where's the old
man?" I said.
"Sleeping still, but he's okay. I think the fever is
gone. He woke up for a few minutes, but he needs
rest. You go wash up; I'll fix some breakfast. Then

you can go home and get some rest. Come back later;
he said he wants to speak to you."

"No," I said. "I'll stay for a while; I can watch him
while you get some rest. He's been good to me, I'll
stay."

Then I got up and went to the washbowl. There
was no water, so I walked outside and worked the
pump until water flowed out into the white bowl.
When I came back inside Rose had breakfast ready.
The table was set with eggs and fried potatoes, fry
bread, strawberry jam and honey. Rose poured
another cup of coffee for me, and we both ate heart-
ily. After breakfast I went out to the front porch to
smoke. The sun had cleared the tallest trees of the
reservation by then, and I could hear voices on the
road to the church hall. As I lit a cigarette Rose came
out and sat down beside me.

"Go inside," I said. "I'll watch the old man as soon
as I'm done here."

She looked out into the trees as wisps of black hair
licked the bones of her chin and grazed the flatness
of her cheek. "I don't know if I can sleep," she said.
"I keep hearing the voices out here, I keep thinking
of my father, this whole place. You know, where
we all come from."

ROSE MESKWAA GEESHIK'S
MONOLOGUE ON IMAGES

Everybody on the outside—at the colleges I've been
to, in the white churches, on the street, in the stores,
superstores, and movies—they claim to know us,
to know where we came from, how we lived, what
we ate, what we produced, even what we believed,
but how many of us are there now? And what do
they know, or care to know, about what we believe
or how we live today? I know, there are some good-
intentioned, sincere singers of sorrow and guilt in
the highest and lowest offices and places of power,
in this well-fashioned world, but few of them can
fathom the cryptic nature of their own concern, genu-
ine or otherwise. For a long time, I saw the irony in
these American vistas from a long way off, in the so-
called first ship coming to discover what was already
here. Then there were the images, the cowboy kill-
ings, the product faces, figures giving authenticity to
their smoke, their Sunday heroes. And for a long
time I swallowed it all and grew sick with anger,
knowing the images inside can kill you and put faces
on you that you can't get off, and it was the old man
inside there sleeping and his companion, my mother,
who washed those angry faces off. They taught me
different, greater things about images, about the
imagination, and growing toward healing. And I
found I could turn images inside out from the mind
to the hand, and the images in turn could replay healing images inside someone.

My first painting came naturally, forming the earth, a turtle, the earth, a civilization on its back. Beyond, beneath, around the turtle, there is nothing but space and remote specks of light, though one great red sun hovers above the turtle. People live on the back of that turtle, part of the earth on the turtle's back is on fire. Some of the people are running into the fire; some are running away. Another part of the turtle's back is ice. Some of the people on earth are sliding off the ice, out into space. Some of the people are freezing to death. Another part of the turtle includes a great forest. In the tallest trees, some people are reaching for the stars; some reach out too far and fall into a river that flows from where fire meets ice. Some people in the forest live inside hollowed-out trees and so they don't know light. The turtle itself has pulled in its legs and head. I know it sounds like a simple painting, but I felt good about it, I had done something.

In time I had a whole collection of those kinds of paintings—on turtle themes. Then I had a great eagle period. I won a State Arts Award for a painting titled "The Nest and the Mind." I know it sounds like a simple concept. But the nest was full of waste, garbage, and the eggs of the eagle were hatching, but they weren't hatching eagles, they were hatching glowing signs, advertisements, human legs and arms, body parts, rusting machinery, flowers on fire, liquor bottles with warped human heads inside at the bottom. The nest sat at the top of a dead tree. People who were born in the nest were trying to get out of the nest; the nest was overflowing and waste and people were falling out; there were mangled airplanes, plastic guns, boys with needles in their necks, girls choking on pearls as they fell from the sky. At the bottom of the tree there were heaps and heaps of dead eagles—golden eagles, bald eagles are piled there on the earth. A white-headed old man sits on a log, watching the eagles fall; he too is painting, an X-ray picture of a fallen nest, upside down on the ground. In his picture, eagles fly, in a bright blue sky above the nest, rising from the heap of dead eagles, circling, as humans inside the upside down nest are engulfed in steam.

After that painting, I made good money selling paintings. I stayed in the Twin Cities at the time, to sell art. Then I met a man from another reservation. His name was Leon Meskwaa Geeshik, and I still go by his name. He treated me well. We talked about all the good things we could do. We talked of returning to the reservation, of creating new political and economic worlds there. In 1969 he was drafted. I told him to go home, to take asylum among his family on the reservation, but he went in with a friend from Little Earth instead. The army put him on reconnaisance. For a while I got letters from him. They weren't about war or death. They were honoring letters of love to the earth, to the reservation, to me, to the memory of Indian people. I still have those letters. I keep them in an old winnowing basket, beneath two ricing sticks. I've never showed the letters to anyone, not even his mother, who still lives in the house Leon grew up in.

While he was gone I couldn't do any art work. No images struck me. I didn't paint for years. Then the letters stopped. I never heard from him, and I was lost. Within myself, I promised to continue with my work, though I had no word of Leon's death or return. I made a plan to set up a studio on the reservation—a place of inspiration. I put the studio on the highest hill, overlooking the mission, east of the housing projects, east of Four Bears village, on the reservation. In one room I put a big picture window, hoping that something outside that window would inspire me to paint another picture. I put a desk in front of the window and I put an easel with a blank canvas next to the desk. I kept a sketch pad and note pads on my desk just in case an artistic image passed by. Outside the window a huge maple held the sun's emergence and ascent in different angles in a florid and barren complexity of branches through seasonal winds. It held the moon's face up in the night as I tried to see the next image or as I tried to sleep. I sat at the desk for days drinking and smoking, sometimes crying with shadows. I rarely saw anyone. One day as I sat at the desk nodding off to sleep, a sparrow hawk flew into the window and broke its neck. I thought of a painting of a bird of prey flying at the image of a tree rather than the tree itself, but I couldn't present the double image to my satisfaction, in sketches or on canvas.

Then one afternoon, near dusk, in early spring, as I picked up my pencil to sketch a picture of an old woman I saw floating in thoughts between waking and sleeping, a stone came through the window, shattering glass, throwing glass shards over my head, flinging glass against my face and arms. Some of the pieces drew blood: I felt it as it rolled down from my forehead onto my eyelids, and I tasted the blood as it streamed down from beneath my left cheekbone to the corner of my lips. I looked out into the brightness and saw nothing. But a few leaves left over from autumn turned in a weak whirling wind beyond the trunk of the maple. And I realized my own image in the glass was gone. The person I had been seeing there through the seasons, without realizing it, had torn out into the spring day with the memory of someone barely recognizing an enduring exterior image in the interior inertia. Then I looked back to the paper and saw some of the broken pieces scattered out onto the incomplete face of the old woman I was sketching. Those pieces magnified parts of her face: one of her eyes appeared larger; part of the shadow on the bridge of her nose whirled out wider and darker; the closed part between her lips opened a bit more. I stood up and walked over to where the stone landed after it came through the window and struck the wooden frame of the easel, knocking the canvas to the floor.

At first I didn't know the source of the stone. And that bothered me since the stone was different, almost perfectly round and painted. The stone felt different in my hands too, like someone had touched it many times before, like it had a human purpose attached to it. Part of that purpose rested, I believed, in the symbols painted on the surface of the stone. A thin band of green paint divided the stone in half. On one half of the stone was an image of a blue man painted against a yellow background; on the other half a white bird rested on its back against a red background. After examining the stone I walked outside to the back of the house where the big maple grew. I looked in every direction. I saw nothing I could connect with the stone.

Later, when I dozed off to sleep with the stone
in my hand, I saw the stone again in my dream.
It spoke to me.

Dire Seer
You of a broken window
Descendant of a finer day
Daughter in search of a greater image
Sometimes stones go through the wrong
    window
Sometimes you move into the wrong
    neighborhood
Not this time
This is a creation stone
A stone from the beginning of time
You may use this stone to create
to sing as a song stone
to tell stories as a story stone
to write as a poem stone
to paint as an art stone.

Somehow I felt good about receiving the stone.
I felt a sense of inspiration. Astounded, I held the
stone in my hand and looked out the window once
again. Still there was nothing I could see. I searched
for signs of movement; I listened for sounds of humans. Nothing came to me. The stone spoke again.

A stone is a gift
with every gift comes
a shortcoming
You must care
for a stranger
at your door

I went to the door, opened the door, and looked out. A little man, about three and a half feet tall, stood before me on the porch. He had a dark complexion, long wild black hair, and thick powerful arms. A deerskin covered most of the upper half of his body, and he wore tanned deerhide on his legs from his waist down to his ankles. On each of his ankles he had strung deer hooves. I invited him in. I brought him to the kitchen table and I offered him a chair. He sat down. I fixed him a big meal and gave him tobacco. He sat there smoking for a long time.

Then I was back in my studio, picking up the stone. As I turned it over in my hand, images came to me immediately, in great waves of people and places and stones. I sketched stone drawings, one after another. I sketched a stone rain falling on a city. I sketched Mount Rushmore and replaced the faces of the presidents with reproductions of cathedrals and the domes of state capitols. I sketched a stone bust of every American president, and each bust had Indian clan symbols emerging from the backs of the presidents' heads. I painted hundreds of stone airplanes flying across a field of stars, each dragging articles of treaties on long banners as they flew. I sketched an image of Crazy Horse's vision of taking a stone into battle. I drew men in a strip club in the city, naked, turning to stone, watching a Gorgon stripper pulling a bag off her head as she unties the last string on her costume. I sketched an obscure Renaissance artist carrying stone tablets on his back. I sketched a black horse on a headstone.

Then there was confusion. In another room the little man was surrounded by bottles and cans, he was up to his neck, wild and drunk. He went berserk,

screaming, smashing chairs, breaking glass, running
from room to room, using metal tools, axes, screw-
drivers, hammers, to destroy, at random, the objects
around me. And then he came for me whirling an ax,
cutting the air, trapping me in my studio, where he
ripped up my canvas, chopped up my desk, split it
right down the middle so every paper on the desk
blew about the room in the turbulence of his fury,
and when he broke the desk the painted stone slid
off, skidding across the room, where it came to rest,
from spinning colors of blended images to a still
painted stone at his feet. I saw the back end of an
ax head striking the stone again and again, light
glancing on the ax head as it struck the stone until
the stone was sand, a small mound of colored sand
mixed with gray sand. I felt tears falling from dream
eyes. I charged violently toward the man with a
sharp splintered end from the leg of my broken easel.
Then I saw him running outside the window, the
easel leg embedded in his chest. I saw him running
in circles, shooting arrows into a clear blue sky.

The dream shifted, to my desk, where an hourglass
with red and yellow and blue and white and gray
sand inside kept time in my dream. The hourglass sat
on a stack of papers, on a stack of sketches; there
were hundreds of sketches. Each time all the sand
passed to the bottom of the hourglass a hand reached
out in my dream and turned the timepiece over, and
each time the hand turned the hourglass over, a
sketch on a sheet of paper rose up lightly in the
absent weight of the timepiece and floated out into
the landscape outside the broken window of my
study. This happened again and again, each time
more quickly, until the last sketch drifted out the

window and wound around in an aimless updraft to the top of the giant maple outside my window. There I saw the little man on a death platform, wrapped up in red material as eagles, vultures, crows swirled about and above him, keening, screeching, cawing; some even singing with human voices a death song I remember and will carry with me to the end of my life.

Four days later a boy came to my house. I found him on my doorstep when I stepped outside to go to town for groceries. He was well dressed in the clothes of a mission student. He wore a clean white shirt and black dress pants. His black hair gleamed, creamed thick, running backward in deep comb tracks from the center of his head and in half circles behind
his ears.

"I'm sorry I broke your window," he said as I motioned for him to step inside.

"Sit down," I said. "There must be more to it than your sorrow. The stone itself is unusual, designed with a purpose."

The boy took the blue chair near the south window. "That's true," he replied, "the stone has a purpose, but I'm not sure, you know, about the whole purpose. I use the stone for hunting. I have this slingshot I carry with me. My uncle made it and he gave me the stone after he gave me the slingshot. I get squirrels, rabbits, small animals, you know, sometimes birds. My uncle, his name is Oshawanung, said the stone was passed down from his father to him, and from his father's father before that, but no one knows how far back the stone goes. As for the painting, I believe some little people gave the stone to our family so many generations ago that even the white man can't understand who the inhabitants of this land were then. That's why the little man is painted on one half. As for the other half of the painting, I can't say."

"What about the window? Why did you shoot the stone this way?"

"I'm sorry about your window," he said. "That too is something I should explain."

OSHAWA'S STORY

Some boys at the mission school have been giving me trouble. I think it started when the nuns chose me to carry the Virgin Mary's crown for the coronation ceremony, during the Assumption of the Virgin. I was selected to carry the crown, and Maria Strawberry was selected as the girl who would place the crown on the Virgin Mother's head. Right away the teasing started: those other boys sang at me every day on the road to school about how I loved the Strawberry girl. They never let up. Instead things got worse, especially when the nuns took the two of us out of class, to rehearse our parts in the ceremony. I think the boys were also a little jealous. Some of them really liked that Strawberry girl.

We rehearsed together day after day for a couple of weeks. At first the nuns made us walk through our parts. They stationed me behind curtains on the gymnasium stage until Sister Violet sang the opening song. Then I walked to the center of the stage where Sister Blodgett had painted a red X on the stage. That X was my stopping and standing and waiting point. When Sister Violet finished her song, Marie Strawberry walked out from behind the curtains on the other side of the stage and met me, face to face, at the red X.

After we walked through the parts with the proper timing to the proper places, the nuns added props, one by one. First, I walked to the red X with a satin pillow and an imaginary crown, which Maria took and placed on the imaginary Sacred Mother's imaginary head. After a few more days, we used a cardboard crown covered with tinfoil. During the last week of practice, on the final day of practice, we used a real crown and a real ceramic statue of the Virgin Mother. We also dressed up in the clothes we'd wear for the coronation. I wore a special coronation shirt of white satin with a golden cross sewn on the left breast. My grandmother, old woman Cold Crow, sewed thunderbolts on the sleeves and red, blue, and black ribbons on the back of the shirt. Marie wore a lacey white dress and a silver, stone-speckled tiara.

During the whole time I never spoke to Marie and she never spoke to me. Each day we drifted silently out of class together, following the two sisters, winding through our parts without speaking. But as we were walking back to class after the final dress rehearsal, when the nuns were out of range of our voices, Marie spoke: "You did good today. I know a lot of these boys wouldn't want to do this, but you . . . you did good."

I didn't know what to say. "Thanks," I said and that was all. I wanted to say more, but the nuns were closer to us by then and we were closer to the classroom. I saw a few of the other boys' faces in the doorway as we approached the room, and their sneers and wild grins kept me from speaking further. Not only that but I didn't know what else to say. Marie's deep brown eyes drew me into another secret side of myself that I didn't mention to anyone. After looking at her across from me each day for weeks, I found myself looking deeper and harder than I'd ever looked at a girl before, and all the singing those other boys did as we walked to and from school came true in my head, I had to admit, as I saw Marie so beautiful, dressed for the coronation.

On the day of the coronation, I spilled chocolate milk on the front of my coronation shirt and made a huge stain right beneath the holy cross. For a few minutes I thought my part in the coronation was over—and in a way that made me secretly more secure—but Sister Violet scolded me and made me take off my shirt in front of the whole class. Then she took my shirt out of the room, out to be washed somewhere. I sat there in class for a long time with no shirt. I couldn't concentrate on anything. I kept hearing laughter behind me. I heard whispering. The sisters glared at me for the rest of the afternoon until Sister Blodgett came in beaming, holding up my clean shirt in front of the class for everyone to see.

The whole gymnasium was set up for the coronation ceremony. There were chairs and tables all the way to the back wall so all the schoolchildren could sit down to feast together with their families before the coronation. After the meal we had some free time, so most of the children ran around for a while while their elders talked over coffee and cigarettes. I saw one of the boys from my class then, Joseph Two Birds, standing up on the stage taunting me as a few other boys huddled down behind him at the center of the stage.

Oshawa loves Strawberry
Oshawa is a sinner
Oshawa naw naw hey yaw naw naw

When the time came to crown the Virgin Mother, the gymnasium settled into quiet, like all that every-

one had to say had been released for the time being,
flying on the backs of winged thought carriers to
where our words are held invisible until we need a
certain thought again. I stood back in my place
behind the red curtain. All the light in the gymnasium went out. Dreams came into my head then. I
saw shapes inviting me through sacred doorways.
Two old people came before me—a woman and then
a man. The woman wore a green skirt and a red
blouse with a shawl with red fringes wrapped over
her shoulders. She walked into the white light at the
center of the stage, where she bent over, reached
down through the stage to the earth beneath the
school. She held the earth clenched in her fist, then
she turned her hand over, opened her palm, and
blew on the dirt. The dirt leaped out, revolved in par-
ticles in the light, struck air, and drifted back toward
earth, where each light particle slowly transformed
into the man, from top to bottom as they sifted down
and fell. Then the woman was gone, and a tree without leaves formed as the man was forming, and when
the man became whole he ascended into the top of
the tree to a point so high that I could barely make
out his shape as he gestured down to earth, where
men and women stood weeping at the trunk of the
tree. When I looked back up to the top of the tree, the
man was gone, and a giant bird hovered just above
his place on a limb as a nest fell end over end from
the tree. I heard whisperings from indefinite sources
in the gymnasium, and words coming out from the
dark rose up to the stage.

"Go," the voices said. "Take the crown to the center now." Sister Violet's voice crawled out of the
quiet as I stepped out from behind the curtain.

I walked out toward the light at the center of the stage, balancing the Virgin's crown with smooth, carefully practiced strides. But when I came to the center, the light shone too bright and the spot with the red X was slick with oil or lard, I'm not sure what it was, but I slipped, lost my balance. As Marie approached my legs went out from under me, I lost the pillow, and my foot struck the base of the Virgin Mother's statue. I rolled over away from the statue, saw the Holy Mother's crown rolling away across the stage as I turned over on one side. Stunned, I stared, flat on my back as the statue of the Blessed Virgin fell over on its side. Pieces of ceramic chipped off when she struck the stage; one struck Maria's leg and drew blood there. We both remained stilled onstage in an eternal moment of fleeting disaster. Instantly, tears welled up in Marie's obsidian eyes, growing from the reflected forms in their lit centers, rolling down her face in silver stagelight drops. One, two, three, four drops fell, landing at her feet where the Virgin Mother's nose lay separated from her face, until Sister Violet and Sister Blodgett burst onto the stage crying and screaming, "Look what you've done. Look what you've done to our Virgin Mother."

A few days later on the way home from the school, the teasing turned ugly. Two Birds and his friends sang a new song, revealing the truth about the disaster at the coronation.

> Oshawa falls Oshawa
> Oshawa falls look
> what he's done to the Virgin Mary
> Oshawa falls Oshawa
> Oshawa falls tears

     from the eyes of Maria Strawberry
     Oshawa slips Oshawa
     Oshawa falls from food on the stage
     mashed potatoes and butter
     Oshawa slips Oshawa
     Oshawa falls breaking
     the statue of the Virgin Mother.

As the boys sang the song over and over again I felt angrier and angrier. But I held it inside until I came home. Then I made a plan to get Two Birds. Later that night I went to the drawer where my uncle kept the painted stone wrapped in leather with six pinches of tobacco inside. I returned to my room and unwrapped the stone. As I examined the stone, felt its warmth, thought about its designs, I remembered back to the day I first held the stone four years before. My uncle told me about it.

OSHAWA'S UNCLE'S STORY

This stone has been passed down in our family for a long time. I'm showing it to you now because your grandfather just gave it to me to keep. When you are older then you can hold the stone for your generation.

Your grandfather claims the stone has gifts. Some stones carry earth histories, stories, songs, prayers, so their stone faces hold memories of the existences of other eras; other beings of the earth, air, fire, and water live on, embedded in shapes, in esoteric formations of strata and substrata, in scopic design and microscopic elementals we can only imagine in our limited view of the exterior stone. Beyond the life inside, the stone was also used to kill. The first great weapons relied on stone to kill. So some stones transport memories of death. This is why I believe the Chimookamon uses stones to hold his name while his body rides in the earth in death. As you see, this stone in my hand has those two sides painted on it. Each side tells its story. A person can use this stone to remember, or turn it over and use it as a weapon. Remembering with the stone will keep you safe in creation, since remembrance opens you up to forms of creation. Thus your safety will reside in your willingness to understand the story of the stone and use the story in the stone to understand and create your own story as you remember the stories of our family, our people.

Now as I hold this stone, I feel a particular pride

in our people, and at this moment, this stone tells me we can't be killed. We can be hurt; we can be changed; we can be consumed by the desires and passions of ourselves and other people; and we can be buried. But as a people we can't be killed. I know because when I was growing up in the old village there was a family living across the road from us in one of those shacks of wood and tarpaper. The head of the family was an old man named Moses Four Bears. He lived in that house with his wife and four children. One winter when I was about sixteen, one of his sons came pounding on the door early in the morning. Both my father and mother were out at the time. Father, I think, had gone to trade some skins for some food at a nearby town. Mother was visiting around the village.

When I went to the door, Four Bears' son said, "Get your father. My father needs your help."

"He's gone," I said. "There's no one else home."

"You come, then," he said.

We crossed the road as an icy wind rose up out of north and west, turning the village white in twisted mists. Inside the shack, the two younger children huddled under blankets near the wood stove while the two eldest girls and old woman Four Bears attended to the old man, who lay stretched out on a sofa. They applied medicine, ground roots, and tobacco, and they dipped cloths in steaming water. The lower part of his leg was gone—the leg was a shortened stump, wrapped in cloth, seeping blood. The cut-off part of the leg sat across the room in a wooden box on a wooden chair.

The old woman spoke as I came into the room. "He drank too much," she said. "Willow"—she raised her head toward her oldest daughter—"found him in that ditch where the sweetgrass grows, around the bend from the liquor store. The foot was frozen, part of the leg too. He had diabetes anyway; if it hadn't froze, it probably would have gone bad. We gave him more alcohol and they cut it off at the clinic in Fineday. I don't know, maybe this will be the end of it. He told us to send for someone, to bury the leg for him."

At that the old man opened his eyes for the first time since I entered the room. "Cut off part of the legging of my dance outfit, from the outfit with the flower and vine work on the lower legging," Four Bears called between clenched teeth. "Put a good moccasin on the foot and then wrap that whole thing up and bring me tobacco."

Willow left the room through the doorway leading to the back of the house. The other older daughter, Esther, drifted over to the table nearby and picked up a wooden bowl from the table against the wall away from the stove. When all was done as said, the old woman brought the leg over and set it down on the floor in front of the couch where the old man lay. The old man rose up to a sitting position, grimacing between words and action. He spoke in the old way, clenching tobacco in his palm. A few tears rolled out with his words, not from pain but from loss and the sincerity of his words, which I comprehended, though I knew only a little bit of the language. When the words stopped he opened his palm and dropped the tobacco into the box, where it fell on the leg in a thin sprinkle. Then the girls wrapped the leg in bright floral-print trade cloth and nailed a lid onto the box.

Four Bears gave me tobacco. "Take the leg out and bury it. But go beyond the cemetery, close to the big river. Just before you get to the riverbank, find a big tree near the bank. Bury the leg there. Take Sonny with you," he signaled with a quick lift of his head and pushed out his lips, toward the boy who sat silently, watching near the wood stove. "When you're done come back here," he said as he lay back down.

The icy wind pulled the door out of my hand and slapped it violently against the house as we went outside. Sonny fought to close the door. I looked back from the road, squeezing the leg into my body with both arms, and saw the boy as a crouching shadow, trudging against the wind to follow me. We crossed the road, stopped back home, and picked out a shovel.

Most of the time the walk to the cemetery doesn't take long. Even when someone dies, the distance is a few miles at most. But the wind ate into the day and spit snow out of winter's whistling mouth in deep, obstructive drifts of cold ghosts, layering a struggle to make it to the burial place with further struggles to make it to nearly invisible landmarks—the one-room library shack of books donated by churches, the bell tower that rang into our Sunday mornings and resonated in our heads as the remembered place of an old priest's flying suicide, the cemetery with all the missing crosses and illegible stones.

By the time we made the cemetery, Sonny looked lost. The wind sang in fear in his eyes. He was too young to go further into the cannibal intensity of that storm, so I told him to turn around and go back home. "I'll bury the leg," I said, taking the shovel. "It's okay, go back."

Then I turned and headed toward the river. I found a tree there, just off the river bank, an expansive birch, an old one. I set the box out and started digging. Under the fallen snow the ground was ice. The shovel bit back in stinging vibrations in my hands as I struck the earth. I struck again and again, but the earth didn't give, and I felt my face and hands flying into the air in numbness. I listened to a voice inside.

Old man Four Bears should have known. You can't do this now. Return the leg to Four Bears. Go back yourself. Sonny will tell them about the cold, this wind. Go back to Four Bears. No, leave the leg; you can't bury this; go back now; find a place for the leg. You'll freeze here if you don't go back now.

I listened to the voice and whirled around looking for a good place on the earth to leave the leg. I saw another tree, big and strong, with barren branches toward the bottom of the bank where the snowed-under earth met the river. I went to the tree and tried to climb up the trunk with the leg under one arm, to another, higher part of the tree, to a place where I could wedge the leg in and lodge it until the storm subsided. Then I thought I could come back and bury it. I did that and headed back.

The whole world was white then. I looked for my tracks on the way back, but the storm covered everything. I had no direction. Places that were so familiar were gone, swallowed by the storm. I kept feeling for my face; I let the shovel fall from my hands, hearing the voice inside telling me which way to go. I stumbled over crosses in the cemetery. I came to the church, imagining the warmth inside, but the big doors were closed and I couldn't get in. I called out, but the wind and the walls of the church consumed my voice, so I went on. Somehow I came out in the back of the library. Again, I struggled to open a door. But snow and cold and wind locked the door. There was no one inside. So I went to the side of the building and punched the window with my numb hands. I struck the window again and again, again and again, until there was space for me to get inside the building.

I fell into the room, my hands bleeding from the broken glass. But even inside, the storm still whirled out. Frigid wind pounded in through the shattered window space, turning papers up on the librarian's desk. A few books fell from shelves with each new blast in the opening in the room. And the room was cold. The old wood stove sat open-mouthed, in one corner, empty, near the only reading table in the place. I thought of fire. I found matches on top of the stove and thought of fire again. I looked down beside the stove, but there was no wood. I covered the whole room seeking wood. I found nothing, so I started on the books. I randomly pulled pages from fallen books that lay strewn about the room. I crumpled the paper and filled the stove bottom. When the fire gained force, I threw in whole books. In time the stove gave off heat and I felt my face returning. It came completely back to me when I felt the pain of the deep cuts in my hand. Then I moved the librarian's desk across the room to a place beneath the broken window. I turned the reading table over on top of that to block the wind.

I made a place for myself then, right near the wood

stove. I went down the wall from the books nearest the wood stove to the books on the shelves farthest away. I stacked up volumes of books there next to me and kept feeding the stove. Some of the books burned for a long time, and a few of those long-burning books together gave me time to break chairs for wood, and then I had time to sleep and read through the storm.

BOMBARTO ROSE
MIXED-BLOOD MUSINGS IN OBSCURITY

The first book I picked up drew me in with its cover. It looked like birch bark, but it felt like leather. And in the center of the simulated tree bark, there was a black-and-white portrait of an evidently mixed-blood man in an oval frame. Under the oval head the title read, in big gold letters:

Mixed-Blood Musings
The Sorrow of the
Impossible
under the Moon of the Improbable
Essays, Poems, and Stories

Beneath that, the author's name spelled out in smaller print:
Bombarto Rose

So I read on, alone in a cramped library of books donated by the various Christian churches on the reservation. I read on in the biggest white storm our reservation ever knew.

Preface
For a long time I've concentrated my complete intellectual attention on echoes of ancestors coursing through human blood. I've metaphorically cut myself to study such blood under the microscope of human relations in human communities. To understand that study one must first understand that blood is both

red and white. These interactive cells fight off disease, coagulate at the skin's surface, oxygenate the physical aspect, and frequent the mineral marrow of the same aspect. What this means, of course, if the blood echoes are correct, is that blood conveys and infuses the basic elements of creation—mineral (earth), oxygen (air), impulse (fire), and liquid (water)—in its force and flow. This vain and worthless study—and a mild case of blood poisoning from a Taiwan-made Navajo-style earring—eventually invited me to impose certain facts on the notion of history. History begins with the implausible conception of the evolution of the interpretation of other implausibles, designated as facts. So I designed a history which rested on the notion that blood must be shed and people must die before history and its mythological impositions can be generated. The secret to the end of the convoluted and question-laden quagmire of a historical thesis I proposed lay in the final sentence of my work *The History of Humankind: Words Written by Blood*. The sentence read, "Thus the historian writes only to find that thoughts rest on the passage of blood through the human body."

Perhaps the critical attention the book received offers reasons for going further. No one read the book, so apparently history has no connection to human blood. Obviously, I couldn't stop there. Clearly, there must be blood if there be thought. But the thought impulses, subsequent to visible and invisible human manifestations of the thought, were left unexamined in my work. If the admixture of earth, air, fire, and water in human form is receptive to the admixture of blood in the resonances of the admixture of animal and human brain, then what happens to the impulse? Does the human receptor in its mineral density conduct the electrical flash so completely in the brain that the whole impulse is swallowed up by the physical form at the time the human thought is transmitted? Or is the conductor weak, and thus only a small portion of the impulse arrives at the point of thought—like a train with more seats than passengers, or like a luminous stone white canoe with an infant orphan passenger who has no language for arrival or departure? Or is there another ground, an external ground which accepts and holds the message outside of the body of thought which produced the impulse? The seeds for my next book—*The Golden Roots of Impulse*—flowered and fructured there until I came to the final chapter and discovered that I lost my train of thought somewhere and had to return to an earlier chapter, "Mystic Revelation," to find out if what I wanted to say lingered somewhere on the pages there, among the marginal notes of my first draft. No such luck. I promptly abandoned the project and returned to the reservation mission where my illegitimate father still lived among other religious fathers.

He was, as you might expect, a gray old man. And as I came into the mission I could not comprehend how he'd grown so old so quickly. Just two years earlier, when I first discovered him, he had seemed bright and extremely well kept. At that earlier point he meant nothing to me; he was like the rest of the fathers there, another father among many fathers, dutifully asserting the Christian faith at an open house for young American Indian men who might be considering a life in the monastic brotherhood. I never suspected that he was my father until he told me so. "My name is Father Milton, but I'm like you," he said, "a man with the same type of blood in my veins."

At that point in our conversation I wondered, was I, an educated mixed-blood Indian, like this man who spoke in clichés? Or worse, did I hide the clichés under a cloak of a different system of language?

"That's good, Father," I said.

"So then you believe," he said.

"Yes, Father," I said. "I believe."

"That is good then. For I am truly your father. Your mother and I met years ago on the reservation during the time when the head father, Brother Defleet, assigned me to deliver the word at the reservation mission church. I first saw her after church, at a water pump. She carried a wooden bucket. As I approached, I saw all of the sky in the water she carried. She was extremely beautiful, as you must know. Her eyes cast a certain demure insignificance that arrested me in a moment, in a mold of dark human desire. Passion flowed between us; love carried me into the abyss no holy father must enter. Ah, but I did, and I knew that someday you, my son, would enter into this sacred space where I could finally relieve myself of the unspoken burden I've carried with me. You are my son." Then he wrapped his arms around me and cried so profusely and wetly that I didn't return to the mission until after I had lost my thought in the last chapter of my work in progress. I returned with a new intention. I wanted to quit philosophizing on blood and human nature and thought, and examine myself in a variety of forms. My father was a natural source for the information and ideas I'd need to complete the project. This is when I saw how conspicuously ancient he was. I found him in the shadow of a decaying autumn garden. He sat on a stone bench twirling the rope of his Franciscan robe around, watching sparrows vacillate between trees.

"Listen," I said as I approached, "you can hear the earth changing. The memory of an old seed sings in these gray winds, coveting a spring of anticipations, quieting a summer recollection."

"Ah, but the heart of the wintering bird still beats at the same pace in the same land," he said.

Then I knew the war was on. I came to the man for information and he engaged me in philosophical dialogues, in poetic musings with all of the eastern and western syncopations, juxtapositions, trophy-hunting tropes two word-wielding angels could muster in the necessary competitive encounters between father and son. The following poems, aphorisms, metaphors, and discourse fragments represent in language and simulated thought personal recollections and manipulated results of the encounter.

Father's Prologue

Henceforth, holy autumnal muses of one
    true God,
damn the deleterious who would
address the spirit with drumbeats,
champion my cause against caustic
    indifference

against he who would charge the material
    of my physical
being with improper propositions,
with pre-Columbian truths,
which even today manifest in the gesture
    and speech
of those you've drawn us to.
Allow me to elevate the tone and tenor of
    my tenuous speech,
into a forceful and holy powerful traffic of
    words.
Allow me to augment the intellectual
    shadow
with a well–lit fatherly ghost,
Allow me to carry the dispensations
of this material world to your spiritual door
that I may speak, that I may utter
the holy profundities the proprietors of
    human passion
must hear as they hear the voice of death
in the somber gray wind
on the way to the cemetery of whirling
    brittle leaves.

Son's Prologue

Oh mystery, oh creator
Earth and sky reside in us
Sun bands cross the villages of our sleep
and the people wake to warm themselves,
in even the coldest of times
with the warmth fire brings.
So it is with the gifts of your creation,

the hands feel warmth, the face comes alive
and the people are charmed
out of their sorrow
for what has gone
or what may never come.

And when our voices are cracked and
    broken
in dryness we have
our spiritual legs or the legs
of others to carry us to water
where we find our faces with clouds,
and sky, sunlight held,
swimming in the depth of your creation.
And all things are together in one moment
as all things are in creation.

This the ancestors remember and so I ask
for their assistance that I may remember
through them in all their varied forms,
trees, grasses, medicine plants, fruit plants,
vegetables, waters, water beings,
two-leggeds,
four-leggeds, winged ones, earth, sky, sun,
those to come, that I may speak properly,
for understanding, for him
who would argue
against the life in all things.

The Father's First Response

A boy came to me once,
worried by a dream.
He said he saw the world on fire.
A woman came to me once,

from a house of dead children.
She said she never wanted to live
to see so much death.
Each in his own way returns to the father.
For the father lived that we may see
fire in our time.
And the father died that we may live.
But the boy never listened
though his dream returned often.
The woman left but flowers for the dead.
Now the father sees them on the road
each day
on the road to kingdom come
and he reaches out and touches them
each day when the day is done
but neither turns, both keep on their way.

The Son's First Response

When you speak of children, of the earth,
of what is man's, you speak as if man were
    all there is.
The woman knows as the child knows the
    child she may carry
as the earth carries us for so many
    numbered suns.
So to speak of only father, to speak of only
    son or daughter
leaves the circle incomplete.
A trinity without the woman denies
the very earth beneath our feet. And this is
    what bears us;
this is what we return to in unity
with remembrance of the father.

The Father's Response
to the Son's First Response

It is true humble beginnings are good for
    people
but humble beginnings lead to greater ends
as great beginnings can only end humbly.
But who would deny a man his sacred will?
Some, in will, see beauty as a great
    flowering tree;
Some see, in will, the circles beyond even
    our brightest star.
Some, in will, remember from wills
    passed on to them
that this life, this earth, is not the end.
Ah, but you speak as if will is a substance
    reflected
back by the substance of the eyes. Clearly
even substance reaches much deeper
into the mind I can see.

The Son's Response
to the Father's Second Response

It's substance you're now seeking to decry
    my way of life, this must mean you
want to know how my world transforms,
as the greatest of your heroes in substance
    on the tree
transformed into a cross upon the wall.
So it is with trees, in the way they grow,
in the flowering, in leaves, the substance
at any moment reveals only aspects
    in the eye.

But these aspects taken to their end
either inside or outside the mind impart
more as in the connection in the invisible
    world
between all things.

The world began amorphously
neither man nor woman
a bringer of darkness
a bringer of light
a shadow of some extra
celestial machinations whirling
off the dying hope
of a dying planet;
sun between sun, before sun,
after star, sun to come
into light, light into air,
into water into gas into mineral.
Science trembles then with such knowledge
man quakes, the earth spins on such
    knowledge
as man buries, darkness follows and the
    form rises
out of earth, slouching from the weight of
    its origins,
the combined weight divesting
from the form when the sun burns long
and hot enough to change
the density of the material world.

The mountains move
man moves to the mountain
a word arrives from on high
to give us the word of all
that has happened beginning to end.

The Father's Final Response

So, form has crossed your mind
again in a metonymical aspect,
a beast crossing through a human drought.
Let us argue of such form
in a form neither of us knows so well.
Let us argue in each other's absence.

Then the old father rose and entered the back door
of the mission church, to prepare for another mass.
And I was on my own again to begin again.

THE AUTOBIOGRAPHICAL PROFILE
OF BOMBARTO ROSE
AN ESSAY ON PERSONAL ORIGINS

I am of two names of two people. My father was a missionary ideologue who set forth on the land of the reservation to lead Native people to accept and adhere to the teachings of his particular Christian orientation.

My mother was Aishkonance—an Anishinabe flower, a descendant of a crane clan man.

The union of these two people occurred outside the force and sway of the culture systems their lives engendered to that point.

I grew outside the world of my father and lived inside the world of my mother.

From seed, people saw me as a secret, but they treated me as a rumor. The people cared for me as a relative, yet they spoke in low tones of my tracks to the womb.

I was born in 1944 in a blue room attended by midwife grandmothers. When I unfolded into this human form, screaming with a violet face for more air, an old woman named Nawgoom sang over me and named me Kin gooshis Ishpeming (Son of Sky). At that moment a military aircraft passing overhead, on its way to a South Dakota bombing range, accidently dropped a bomb on the reservation. Fortunately, the bomb did not detonate. Still, the shell embedded deeply into the earth, where it remains to this day unexploded, a harmless empty experimental shell, as the military experts explained later. So the bomb that fell on the day of my birth became part of my other name, Bombarto. The *-arto* part of that name stands for "are too," which means, I gather, that I am also, or I am too, or in addition to the name given me by Nawgoom, I am what happened on that day as well. As for the Rose of my surname, that came from the people as well when they heard that on the day of my birth for the first four years of my life, someone left a rose at the tribal post office for my mother. I believe the rose came from the mission—the only place where people grew flowers.

I went by that name all my life, in school, out of school, beyond the death of my mother, when she was asphyxiated in a blue Nova. The car skidded off an icy winter road and rolled into a ditch as she and her six sisters drove back from church bingo in a town outside the reservation. Apparently, they left the engine running to keep warm until help arrived. But the tailpipe of the car stuck in the snow, so the fumes backed up. Old man Geeshis found them the next morning on his way to a horse auction. The county sheriff told me the whole story later that day as he handed me my mother's purse. When I went through her wallet I found five hundred dollars. She'd won big at bingo. I took the money and left for the cities.

I lost a few days then in mourning, in dreaming, on Franklin Street, in bars, drunk in a corral of flying faces, in housing projects. I connected with cousins and old schoolmates and left my sorrows in conversations I don't recall, but by which people still remember me.

What I do remember of that space I recall in parts as I recall the "Prisoner of Haiku," the story of a prisoner passed on to me in an urban Native village by an Anishinabe recruitment officer from a substantial university.

THE PRISONER OF HAIKU

He never saw himself as a prisoner, at least as far as I can know. And of course he carries another name, but I use the name "the prisoner" as a reference to the years he spent in prison for idealistic crimes. He received ten years for burning down liquor stores, federally funded enterprises, and other imposing white structures, on and around the Fineday Reservation. Apparently, he lost his voice many years before that in a distant government boarding school. A few teachers in the school didn't like the way he continuously spoke his own native language in school, so they punished him. Two strong men with the force of God and Jesus, who knows what else, dragged him outside on a bitter wind-chilled Minnesota day and tied him to an iron post. They left him then without food, without water, through the night. Somehow the men believed that the force of the cold, the ice hand of winter, would reach out and take the boy by the throat and silence his native language. The other boys looked out the windows of their quarters, but they saw only tree shapes through snow slanting, as far as the light of the building let their eyes reach. Even so, they heard the punished boy screaming in defiance all night, defending the language, calling wind, calling relatives, singing, so he wouldn't forget. The screaming went on all night, and in the morning, on a bright winter day, when the school fathers went out to untie him, the boy could speak no more. No matter how fiercely or how often

they beat him, the boy would not, could not speak.
The teachers' tactic worked on the boy: he no longer
spoke his native language. But the punishment went
further, deeper, than the imposition of social stric-
ture: the boy couldn't speak English either. When he
opened his mouth to try, less than a whisper stirred
air in an inaudible act of diminished physical volition.
Boys who were close to him then said that though
they heard nothing, they felt something: a coolness
floated out of his mouth and went directly to their
ears to the point where—the boys claimed—their
hearing was frozen in time. That is, though they
walked away from the boy with the frozen words,
they felt the breath-held syllables melt in their heads
later, in words of the Anishinabe language, and still
later in Native translations of circumstances and relationships that they never would have thought of
without remembering the cold in their ears. Moreover, boys who went to the same boarding school,
years later, testified to hearing Native words whirling
up with every snow from sundown to sunrise in their
winters at that place.

I know this: I slept in the ruins of the boarding
school last December, waiting four nights for snow,
and I heard the voice of the boy. What was spoken is
untranslatable, immutable, subject to semantic contexts of pain most people can't fathom in the world
in which they hear and speak. Yet the voice had a
strength, a powerful resilience.

As for the boy, he drifted back to the reservation,
where he became a silent man of hands, a sculptor,
then a political artist, an invidious communicator of
visual forms. He made a living that way until he
turned to acts of sabotage, for him another form of

art. For the sabotage was never performed without
the grace and idealism of an artist. When he burned
liquor stores, when he burned federally funded structures, he mixed flammables so magnificiently that the
buildings burned in colors and fireworks that left the
reservation and nearby communities gasping "oh
(incredulous) mys." One time his fire left a smoke
that drifted into the shape of a human face. People
who saw it swear the face was of an old one, the first
bringer of light, or of one who floated in a stone
white canoe. On another occasion, his fireworks
illuminated the night with the words "The treaty of
1837." On the night of his greatest political burning,
on the night of his seventh fire, on the night in which
the flames reached up, exploding bottles, licking the
dark with colors and room cracklings, on the night
people gathered to see in the flames an old lodge,
ancestors within the lodge, throwing melted clocks
into the air, burning the country-and-western ambi-
ance of chairs and wall hangings, pointing to the
melting jukebox, singing instead healing songs
through that wasting machinery, to tell the people
the lodge is still open—on that night the FBI found
the silent man and arrested him among his cache of
art materials in an abandoned barn near the state
game refuge.

What could he do? Speak in his own defense? Nod
his head with his hand on the Bible and convey the
truth in a series of still lifes, or antlered sculptures,
for a jury who didn't understand his artistic aims? For
a jury who had been selected by two lawyers, one of
whom would represent him without knowing what
he could say? He resorted to one last symbolic act.
He made a shirt and painted the words "guilty" and

"not guilty" on the front and back. Then just before he entered the courtroom, he put a cigarette in his mouth, gestured to his lawyer, and pointed at the tip of the cigarette. When the lawyer gave him a light, however, he took off his shirt and crushed the tobacco of the cigarette onto the shirt and set it on fire with his lawyer's lighter. He went to Deepwater Prison after a one-week trial.

For years prison meant a series of drawings to this artistic warrior. With the permission of prison officials, the man made a series of historical murals on the walls of his cell. After two years and a few changes in the mural, prison officials pushed for inmate education. A lovely white humanist came into the school and taught a class on Oriental poetry. She explained the conceptual foundations of such work, the cultural orientation, the affinities between form and image, between isolation and universal vision. She taught the prisoners how to read and write haiku. The political artist adopted the form and wrote graceful passages, which he passed on to the professor one evening before class. The professor carried the works with her on the commuter train the next morning and wept thick silver tears on a brown autumn day as the train passed through smoking urban neighborhoods. She advocated the prisoner's release, based on the beauty of his words. She passed his words on to poets and scholars, lawyers and radical political activists and the prison board. "The unusual nature of the man's crime," she was informed by the prison board, "stems from his unusual methods of producing forms which illustrate his personal conceptions of beauty, and to release him on the basis of his ability to produce beautiful

words might reinforce his use of art to commit philo-
sophically grounded crimes."

For the final week of class the professor prepared a
lesson aimed specifically at the Native prisoner. She
introduced the class to translations of tribal dream
songs. According to her, these songs carried the
same intense brevity of some haiku and Zen koans.
She hoped to make a connection for the prisoner: he
could write haiku and they could be like dream songs
for him; a culturally, politically appropriate act could
be generated in a foreign form, from language to
language, image to form. Obviously, the professor
didn't understand the nature of the Native prisoner's
criminal acts. What she hoped the prisoner would
understand in the relationship between haiku and
dream songs was deeply embedded in the prisoner's
history. A partial loss of language, new forms, old
forms were part of his existence before the professor
gave him a final farewell kiss. This was the last connection she made with the prisoner, since she failed
to win his release. But the time in the class, the education the professor had given him, inspired the prisoner to write haiku and dream songs. And he wrote
only in those forms, as he understood those forms.
When he wrote letters home, he wrote haiku letters;
when he wrote prison officials he wrote in the language of dream songs; when he wrote editorials in
Indian newspapers he wrote haikus; when he wrote
old girlfriends he wrote in one form or the other. This
went on for two years and became the prisoner's only
form of communication. Still he could not speak.

Then, through a cultural coup, a group of Native
advocates for religious freedom convinced state
prison authorities to allow Native spiritual leaders

to come into the prison and conduct traditional ceremonies. Since the education program had been scrapped, the officials agreed. For over a year spiritual leaders came into Deepwater to discuss Native culture and perform ceremonies. One elder spoke about oral history and prophecy; another discussed dancing and drumming; one talked of prayer and the sacred pipe. A fourth elder brought the sweat lodge into the prison. In time, the elders and one or two helpers from the outside conducted monthly sweat lodge ceremonies for the prisoners.

The Native prisoner participated in the ceremonies from the beginning. But in the first lodge, when it came his turn to speak, another inmate had to explain to the elder, Samuel Little Boy, that the man could not speak, that he would pray in silence and pour water on the rocks, then pass the water bucket to signify the end of his personal prayers. At the end of that first sweat lodge ceremony, Little Boy spoke to the group, outside the lodge. "This man," he said nodding toward the prisoner of haiku, "he had to pray in silence here. And I know his story, why he doesn't speak, why he's in here, in this prison. A little while ago after we came out he handed me a note and he gave me tobacco. He wants to speak again. So in one month we will begin healing sweats for this man. Offer prayers for him until that time."

When Little Boy returned a month later, the sweat went on as planned, but the voice didn't come back then. So the group went on with Little Boy sponsoring one sweat a month, and each time they prayed for healing for the prisoner who could not speak. After three more ceremonies he spoke, but the words were brief and breath soft.

The earth embraces
in song the blue sky
moves one face after another.

Apparently, the healing wasn't complete. And after
four more healing sweats nothing changed. The prisoner spoke, but briefly, softly, always with the same
syllabic rhythm, always in strange poetic words.
Finally, another prisoner who had been in the poetry
class remembered the haiku and the dream songs,
and he realized those were the forms the man spoke
in. When one of the Indian prisoners informed Little
Boy about the ways and reasons for the political artist's speech, Little Boy suggested that the healing
sweats continue until the prisoner could speak freely,
beyond the limits of the literary forms he'd learned.
Four more sweats produced nothing more, and Little
Boy never came back to the prison. A Native newspaper ran Little Boy's obituary in January. He died
on New Year's Day bringing wood into his home
on the Fineday Reservation.

No other elder picked up the spiritual traditions
program for the Deepwater prisoners, and the Native
prisoner spoke only in haiku and dream songs.

I made a point to find the man, to read his words,
to hear his voice. Four years after he was granted
parole, I met him on the reservation, at the Strawberry Inn bar. It took some time for me to adjust
my vision when I entered the bar, but when I did my
first glances stopped just short of amazement at the
Indian artifacts and artwork decorating the place. Old
photographic prints and drawings hung on the walls
above booths at the rear end of the room. A variety of
red pipestone pipes hung above the bar, reflected in

a wide mirror behind a stand of hard liquor. Some pipes were carved into animal shapes of eagles and buffalo; some had plain red bowls with carved twisted stems; some stems were ornamented with feathers and beadwork. On both sides of the mirror simulated treaty documents covered the wall in glass cases. Human clay figures, about a foot tall—each unique, in facial feature and physique, each marked with an engraved pictograph on the forehead—lined shelves above the treaties. Except for the bartender, there was only one other person in the place. He sat drinking at a stool, a few feet from a murmuring juke-box, examining the positions of balls on a pool table.

I spoke first. "I know you," I said. He looked my way for a moment, then lifted the bottle between his legs. "I'm here to see your writings, your drawings. I want to put them into a book." I went on. "I've talked to your brother, he said he would let you know that I was coming to see you."

> When the church bells ring
> the road to Rush Lake breaks off
> one cold crow calls there.

That was all he said before he got up from his stool and walked away. I didn't understand the meaning of it until later, when I watched the smoke gliding away from an introspective cigarette. I met him the next morning on the road to Rush Lake. He handed me a birchbark bundle and walked away on the road to the old grave houses.

HAIKU AND DREAM SONGS
OF ELIJAH COLD CROW

The red horse eats
from blowing weeds in human
indulgence at dusk.

The river with a
missionary's name wears an
ice face at dawn.

Walls leave no company:
a man's shadow grows solitary
moon songs in a cell

So many sundown dogs
improvise on a bark fugue
running for machines

Names travel autumn
wind under the formation
of white cranes passing

Flammables in air
sculpted moment to moment
a heart hungry for home

A sky full of shapes
animals of days above
animals below

A dried flower lifts
then you too are gone away
wind over concrete

Let the girls sleep deep
in dandelion grass, let boys
explode from their skin

An old woman cries son
under uniformed photographs
the red hawk keens out

A leader mouths peace
on the bright road from Yellowhead
one thousand trees fall

Who will sing for whom
when he who sings for no one
must die singing

An old dancer whirls
on his bustle feathers shake
surrounding a cracked mirror

What has fallen to earth
this time has fallen to earth
in a whole fog.

Deer measures silence
between words and guns going off
again and again

The road to eternity
is closed by x's and y's
a roof between the eye and cloud

Prison guards sleepwalk
in a cancerous vista
of domestic quarrels

Travelers come out
of sun looking for Indian-
made real crafts real cheap

This one-eared woman
whose father slept with crow once
saw him turn to steel

The sweet upside-down
cake the radical's wife made
changes the dialogue

Anger comes and goes
one fire ant walking the tongue
to the back of the head

Tired of windows
the dull dead dream of cities
Santa Claus lights go out

Eagles nest in the refuge
uncle returns from Vietnam
a drunken shortstop misses a pop fly

A museum with two doors
one door out into the rain
a dark full bus leaves

He of the golden hand
metallurgical carnivore,
carnival god of grease

and meat grows great
until trickster finds
his racing heart.

Oh, you must agree
the words will hold to the end
meaning what they must

Save the fish with beer
one can funds anti-Indian
underprivileged drunks

Now the blue heron moves
striding twice over wet stones
lifting, twisting snakes

Two old ones in this
doorway of light calling come
down come down come down
from that high wall

Two crows rise from a
squashed possum breakfast
cawing in sun bands

Lips to skin under
squash-blossom necklace the day
holds no more for us

Bezhig, neezh, Andaykug
Awkeewanzee neeba, gee
weesinnin wabun

Church women speak out
Flower drives a new galaxy
to her father's funeral

Under the iron tracks
through dwindling space of closing eyes
(a bridge of painted names and years)

Then mother reaches out
picks up the golden cross on
the red formica table

Winter comes for her
sings her death in the guild hall
a boy receives a blanket

In the moon of the
frozen doorknob, what looks good
takes part of your tongue

With many fathers
I leave my voice of the past
not speaking is not not knowing

Hands gesture open
the space around the stone form
man, woman, child

Descended from stone
before the merging of clans
into treaty bands

In black and white, words
coordinates, rivers, lakes, mark
lines over red earth

Signatures, names, the
undersigned, with marks and lines
anglicized in print

Clan leaders, head men
scripted identities so
many with an x.

Andayk, Flatmouth, Sweet,
Minogeshig, Broken Tooth,
an x by the name.

On 59 a moose
lopes through wisps of prairie snow
lost but not afraid

Tracks of birds in dirt
hieroglyphs around stumps are
filling with warm rain

An oar in water
a hand lit by moonlight
journeys holding sky

The dream x of man
the woman in the chromosome
shadow into light

Smell of autumn smoke
trachoma drags away a child
in a fevered village

Name energy repose
before the blue gun reports
death on a distant hill

Winter lasts and kills
and graves can't be dug
by ordinary hands
with ordinary shovels

The heart runs on from an
essential terror, the news is
there is always news

Days are numbered
like numbered suns
sunlight gestures
into dust to a picture
near a radio

The dream x, old man
an Ojibwa at a station
waiting for his wounded son
an American shadow

Bear ascends the stairs
one golden glass from oblivious
to women problems

A boy painted himself
white and ran into a river

A boy painted himself black
and fasted out in the sun

A boy painted himself
yellow and rolled in the mud

A boy painted himself
red and white and black and yellow

Crossing Wind's stick is
invisible at the Megis Lake drum

Abetung he who
inhabits his X mark
in the presence of _____.

BOMBARTO ROSE
ESSAY ON PARAMETERS OF RESIDENCE

The signature X signifies a validating name or the validation of the document. Parameters governing behavior and space precede the X; thus the apparent conclusion is that the X represents an agreement to the proposed parameters. Further factors of space, behavior, and an open continuum of time are delineated in the text of the document. At every point, then, the signature X is held up in dimensional existence as one validating personality for authentic transaction with other validating personalities. Yet the factors—except for time, which we will get to later—are transhistorical beyond the validating moment, beyond the validating personality, beyond even the vested power of the validating personalities. This carries back to the notion of time. The time of the validation of the transactions is recorded so that the transhistorical nature of the continuum of the transaction may be validated by a static historical reference point, such as an X at one end of time. But the other end of time is ahistorical, referent to the natural world, or natural time, "so long as the rivers flow, and the grasses grow." (This is like saying until the lights go out, but without the same natural certainty.) So a known event marked in a historical moment must validate an unknown future based on an incomplete, open-ended (at most), multifaceted (at least) continuum known as time.

Moreover, articles of the document specify behavior on the part of one validating party. Yet in many

cases this behavior is subject to invalidation at some
unknown point by some future unknown personality
who represents a possible end to that behavior, "subject to the discretion of the president." In addition,
outside the scope of additional possibilities for invalidation of the document, other parties have gathered
an implicit presence in the document in that the representatives of the validating authority, on one hand,
in fact represent a legal appendage of the highest ini-
tiators of law for the validating authority. The time
continuum, then, can be cut through by the power of
one validating party and thus deny the continuance
of specified behavior delineated by the articles of the
document. Moreover, the articles engender a historical relevance which determines the content of the
articles. So each article in the document reflects a
historical moment which rests upon momentary
conceptions of the value and authority of the goods,
services, and authorities involved in the validation
of the document. Again the continuum snaps here
in the face of time. The relevance of each article is in-
determinable at the open end of the continuum. To
give one party a blacksmith, or barrels of salt, gives
temporal value of temporal services and goods. The
transhistorical nature of the document breaks down
the duty of behavior specified in each article. (This
happens in language as well as in the values of goods
and services passed on through the validating
document.)

On the part of the other validating party, behavior is most apparently limited to refusal to fight and
residence in designated space or parameters of residence. Since the parameters of residence developed
out of landmarks and numerical coordinates of a

given historical moment, it might be said that the
parameters of space set forth in the documents
evolve into nothing in the time continuum as well.
On the contrary, space involves specious conceptualization of external parameters. Such conceptualization of such space grows from internal possibility of
infinite speculation. Thus space grows from the limitless bounds of human understanding to concretized
physical parameters. Thus, unlike the time continuum, the space factor devolves from the most general
infinite human imaginings to the most particular
physical space. And unlike the time continuum,
which by the document specifies a particular moment
on one signature end and specifies no particular
moment on the other end, the parameters of residence specify certain space at a certain moment on
one end by a devolving act of imagination created by
the physical space which set up the continuum of
time. Thus the space of the document is holy beyond,
before time, named by convenience to solicit an
agreement in language, with predecessors outside
this whirling world dreaming up more words than
there is time to hold in the space of a moment.

Moreover, the artificial residential parameters set
out by the document create a boxlike effect. Thus the
space is limited, unlike the deep language of the articles of agreement, which in almost all cases follow
the parameters of residence. Clearly, the validating
party represented by the X signators may reside in
the box of words for a while, but their resourceful-
ness and their refusal to be limited by the box space
will probably generate deeper, more expansive inter-
pretations of the articles of the document. Some of
the words of the document were not confinable to the

parameters of residence; the box could not hold in words or behavior. Yet many of the residents of the box are identified according to the space of the validating document. This leads to the concept of the artificial parameters of a metaphysical residence.

Religions are informed by a home, a temple, a metaphysical construct which at some juncture becomes inalienable from the divine religious body (as in, "I am _____, from _____"). So the members of the sacred body may live outside the physical space while living inside the metaphysical construct of religious symbols. This concept is important to the creation of the validating document, since the time continuum and the space factor therein collide in language and explode into historical circumstances which have nothing to do with the original historical moments or predocument speculation. The question becomes, then, how does the space become holy? The space becomes holy in its existence before the historical time and through time, by transpiercing the language of the document, generation after generation, since each generation understands and learns to live off the natural and metaphysical bounty of the space. The time continuum of the document, however, remains abstract, rarely referred to in day-to-day survival; moreover, the document itself is abstract, a function of the language, of a historical moment which is rarely referred to except to retain rights to holy space or identification with the space.

BOMBARTO ROSE
A NOTE TO HOLD THE EYES

The dream X draws us on. I cannot speak for Cold Crow, but his words have forced me from the page. I see how he returns to old forms, and in my references to documents I hammer away at myself for thinking of myself, and an old drunken shadow builds another wall. In the dark I look for my hands and find windows beyond the fringes of light around my fingers. On the road a few memories wander away singing, their tracks filling with falling snow. This is who I am, a few photographs taken for a moment of truth, a few belongings wrapped in brittle paper, a few dead relatives away from my own road into the sun. And I don't want to think of Cold Crow anymore. He died where we all die, on the way to death, run down by a vehicle out of control. I went to find him on the road where he gave me his haiku manuscripts, and I found him there, frozen in a ditch, beyond wild wheel tracks. He was the subject of his own name, covered with winter crows feasting on his body. Of course they whirled away when I discovered him; of course I discovered him when they whirled away in great numbers. He had no eyes then. What I had to ask him ran wild with tears from my own eyes. "Cold Crow," I said to the dead body, "I understand now your name. I understand the dream songs, the haiku attempts. I understand this frozen road; the words will come back. They will return from the air and re-form on distant lips." But Cold Crow had no lips; these too were taken by the

voracious birds in a thousand bloody painful kisses.
So I looked to the rest of the body. Everything was
there. One hand rested on one breast, the fingers of
that hand pinched at the tips, near an opening in his
long black coat, as if Cold Crow stopped in oratory,
gesturing to his heart as he referred to some deep
truth without words. But there under his hand,
inside the coat, were words on yellow notepaper.

A Final Dreamsong

a note to hold
the eyes open a hole
in the Fineday earth

make an x in the snow
where you saw me standing last

I am on this road
to town to find a gun
for my lips

make a circle in the snow
a prayer offering of tobacco
make this place
a prayer place
to each of the four directions

put flags of different colors
when the wind turns warm.

BOMBARTO ROSE
WINTER SONG

Winter's movement is the music of sleepers. I pray
and leave tobacco. I turn to the road. I drag the body.
Beyond the grave houses, further back in the bush, I
find a house of stories, a shelter from ice and wind. I
leave the body outside as the old woman watches me
through a small square window in a door.

Inside Cold Crow's one-room lodge, his mother,
an old woman, sits on an old iron bed. I stand just
inside the doorway. She reads my face for age, for
something beyond what I can tell her. She motions
for me to sit in a weak wooden chair near the wood
stove. I rest my eyes on the floor as she speaks.

OLD WOMAN COLD CROW'S MONOLOGUE ON THE DEATH OF HER SON

The lines of age tell the storyteller's death,
in a fire on the road from the eye to the
    mouth
that words couldn't put out.
Some of us are not given to words.
We gather our strength from shapes,
dead forms on windblown hills, dead
forms in white ditches,
descended upon by wild birds.

Once a hunter returned home, dragging
the weight of a dead animal,
carrying a steaming heart on a stick;
"Eat with me," the hunter said,
"of the heart first."

And now, you, a stranger in so many ways,
come into my lodge, dragging
some dead man behind,
a man with no eyes a man I know, a man I
knew might come to this death,
and you want me to speak
of this shape as his hunter father
asked me to eat part of the heart.

This man, my son
This man, my son
his pain came out of a desire to dream of
    better ways.
But he did not see the dream;

he did not let go of desire.
He walked away from this door one day,
    with a stranger
who took him away
to the mission school
to the mission school on the hill
near the mission church
near the mission cemetery.
This man is my son.

The heart still dripped blood;
when I ate it,
it was not bitter; it was not sweet;
it tasted of fullness,
of mineral, of liquid,
of plants the animal must
have ingested in its days.

And you want to know something of this
    man.
I have nothing to give you.
Your face shows the face of a seeker
and in this man who lost his voice,
in this man who turned silence to beauty,
beauty to human action, you've found
    nothing
but a form for your own search for some
    intellectual truth.
Perhaps like him you have entered
one too many schools, where people
tried to disclose how to speak,
what to think, what is worthy of desire,
even the name of the creator;
and you came out of such places looking

for yourself or looking
for a road to take you home.

Take a story with you then.
Consider it payment on a request,
so you will help bury my son
and you will help me carry out his
request for a prayer offering
at the place where he was last seen
    standing.
I know that place.
It rests on a high hill
overlooking Megis Lake.
When we are finished here,
we will bury Elijah there.

OLD WOMAN COLD CROW'S STORY AS
PAYMENT TO BOMBARTO ROSE

A young man's father
liked to look at himself when he was
   young.
Wherever he went he sought his own face
or shape in mirroring details around him.
When he was young and wild, he would go
to water to pray, or so people thought.
But no, he went to see himself
reflecting on the surface of the water.
This looking grew in him.
When metal objects came into his hands,
he looked for his hands or face there,
or when he passed windows, he often
   stopped
to examine the boy in glass.
In time, relatives saw this happening,
but they did nothing to stop it.
Many people felt he would grow beyond
this interest in his own shape,
to see beyond to greater things.
Well, he quit looking at himself in
   everything,
but no one knew because people grew
   accustomed
to looking at him, looking at himself
in a certain way. And people assumed what
he once saw he always saw, or what he
   once looked for he always looked for.

While he still stopped at glass,
while he still peered into rivers and lakes,
and all the kinds of things he once did,
almost like it was habit,
Only he knew he wasn't seeing
the same thing he once saw.
He saw different things each time:
in one reflection he saw
the way he used to be,
as he wished for a younger self;
in another he saw what he wished to be,
as he wished for an older better self;
in another reflection he conceived of
    himself
as part of a wider image of all
those objects in the mirroring space.
In time his reflections required
no reflecting object.
He saw reflections without turning
his head or moving his eyes.
Sometimes he saw maps or words
and these created reflections for him.
One night in darkness,
just before he rolled away into sleep
he saw a hand before him.
The hand lifted him and set him down
far away in an academy full of strangers.
He learned to make sculptures there and he
    did this:
He learned to take a piece of the earth
and shape it and fire it to hardness,
into lasting unchangeable forms.
At first he gave the sculptures away as gifts.

When he returned home he handed out
     sculptures
all around the village.
Even when he disappeared,
his sculptures kept showing up.
I have one of those sculptures;
it shows a man on a red horse.
Before he went away he said,
"This sculpture tells a story."

ABETUNG'S STORY

My father was Abetung and his father was Abetung and so on back to the earliest inhabitants of this place. I tell it this way, so that these words will have weight in relation to my relations and in relation to the words they inhabit through the names of my relations. My mother was of the Two Birds family, though her father signed his name Lightning and her mother signed her name Tree. Beyond that I know there are Seeds in her family, from a long time ago.

As for the sculpture and the story of the sculpture, if you look closely at the horse you see that the rider doesn't really have control, and that is part of what the story means.

Old man Geeshis, who lived near our family, was going away, and he asked me to stay and take care of his house and feed his horse while he was gone. I agreed. Before he left he gave me instructions. Whatever you do, he said, don't ride that horse. Chibai is not used to strangers and I don't know how he'll react.

I followed his advice for a few days, but I couldn't resist trying out the horse. Late one night I went out back of his house to see the northern lights. The sky shown like I'd never seen it before and the galaxies and constellations shined out in depth of darkness beyond, vibrating green and blue wisps of ancestral dancers on the northern horizon. In a strange way I felt the power and magnitude of the depth of space, even though the northern lights brought the sky clearer and closer than I'd ever seen it before. As I took in the power of this sight, I heard the horse off in the distance whinnying and singing out. I went back to the horse's stall and whispered and stroked it, but the horse kept on with those eerie ghostly cries. The horse song and the sky put a fear into me and I wanted to get away from that place, which at that moment illuminated all the mysterious power I'd ever known. So I whispered to the horse, "Be calm," as I opened its stall and hopped on its back.

The horse quit screaming and calmed a bit as we settled into a slow trot on the road to Bad Medicine Lake. Then a car roared up behind and honked and the horse spooked and shot off into the night, running in fear. I pulled on the reins, screamed Indian and white horse commands loud and often, but the horse kept running. On this winter night the roads were cold and frozen, and I saw disaster at the descent of an upcoming hill. Sure enough the horse ran out of control to the bottom of the hill, where its legs whipped out from underneath us and we skidded into a snow bank beside a shallow frozen marsh. It didn't take long to understand we were stuck. The horse couldn't move from the snow and I couldn't get myself out from underneath the horse. The night grew colder, and soon I lost feeling in most of my body. Then I heard an engine revving as an invisible vehicle made the same disastrous descent the horse made with me. Like the horse the automobile, the source of the engine sound, skidded out of control, whirled around on the road in a weird blend of chaotic lights and roaring metal, and smashed into the marsh just a few feet beyond us. In the darkness I made out the shape of a woman in the driver's side of the car. She was alone. I called out a few times, but she did not move. Time passed and I thought she was dead and I thought it wouldn't be long before I was too. I must have fallen asleep then, because just as the sun came up I looked over into the car and saw the woman looking back at me, through a space she had cleared through the frost on the passenger side window. I motioned to her to roll down the window, but she shrugged her shoulders and shook her head. I gathered the windows were frozen. I also saw in the daylight that the car was lodged door deep into the frozen marsh. So we were both stuck. The worst part was she was far enough away that between the distance and the closed windows of the car I couldn't make out her words when she tried to talk to me.

Time passed and she started writing in frost as a way of communicating to me. The first thing she wrote was *Are you all right?* I shook my head yes at the same time as I wondered where my feet and legs had gone. *Someone will come soon,* she wrote. *Yes,* I nodded, knowing she was being optimistic beyond words. After a few attempts at communication this way, we realized that our conversation was limited: her written communications were limited only to the space of a window of frost; my responses to her writing were limited to yes or no, or simple thoughts relayable only by gesture. As we communicated in this way, the day grew warmer as the sun drew higher. At the sun's zenith, the intensity of our communication somehow turned into an attraction that I knew would save the both of us from freezing to death. Such thoughts created a warm fire of hot impulse in my head. In a warm glowing room and all, I saw myself with this woman, dreamy-eyed, living

out a long human life together. Then there in the
frost I read her message, *Do you like me? I like you very
much.* I nodded yes four times—to leave no doubt
in the silence between us. Apparently the response
got through, since she wrote on the frosty window:
Will you come with me when this is over?

After hours in the sun, some miracle of warmth
and melting ice set upon me and I felt I could move.
At first I twisted a bit in my place and wriggled out of
the snow enough to gather enough leverage to drag
my legs from beneath the horse. Still I felt nothing in
those distant appendages. But on the strength of
arm, and through twist and turn of body, I slowly
crawled over to the yellow car and lifted myself up to
window level. When the woman and I were face to
face, glazed images in ice, she rubbed the glass from
inside, clearing the ice face, clearing the winter cast
from her face and I saw the eyes, the nose, the lips,
the woman inside the vehicle so clearly that I knew
what disaster brought. And I furiously reared my
head back and struck the window with the weight of
my head time and time again until I saw blood on the
winter glass until I felt blood roll into my eyes until
the window shattered the glass appearance of the
woman and brought the real woman within reach.

Once I saw inside I knew why she had not moved.
There was another body in the car with her, draped
across her legs unmoving. "He's dead," she said.
"I tried to wake him but he's dead and I can't
move him."

I fell exhausted to the ground, calling out as I fell,
"Who is he?"

"His name is Franklin Squandum," she said, crying. "He is my brother Squandum. I picked him up in

town at the bus station. He was coming back home
for the first time in four years. He's back from
Vietnam."

"He's big," I said, as I looked into the car once
more. "He must weigh a good three hundred
pounds."

"Yes," she said. "He gorged himself for two years
after the war. I can't get him off me."

"Hold on," I said. "I'll start working on the door."

So I rolled over onto my back and took off my
heavy silver end-of-the-trail belt buckle and hacked
and hammered at the ice and the snow around the
yellow door. In time, as the woman pushed with all
her might from the inside and as I pulled from the
outside, we opened the door wide enough for me
to crawl into the car and free her from the weight of
the corpulent Squandum. Then we were both free—
though she could move her legs and I couldn't—and
so we crawled out of the car to the side of the road,
where I collapsed. When I woke, Mary Squandum
was talking to me while she lay on my legs to keep
me warm. "You'll make it," she said.

Soon a car came onto the road. As it ascended the
hill I saw old man Geeshis driving. He pulled over
when he saw us, and he and Mary dragged me into
the back seat. I immediately closed my eyes and went
to sleep. I didn't want to tell Geeshis about Chibai.

When we got back to the old man's house he built
a fire in the wood stove and he and Mary dragged me
to a place on the floor near the fire. As Mary worked
my legs, Geeshis filled me with warm teas and bitter
remedies I never caught the name of.

Then he said, "I will go get help, to get Mary's
brother out of the ditch. She told me the whole story

while you slept. Maybe someday you will tell me, Abetung, what made you get on that horse. I don't know. Sometimes it seems like words have no meaning to you young people. You go in the direction you want whenever you want without thinking, without believing anything but what your simple passion suggests. But who knows, maybe you took that horse for a reason. Maybe you saw these Squandum people in the eyes of the horse. I don't know. Only you can judge what happened."

With that Geeshis left, and though I felt his anger in his words and his disappointment at the loss of his horse, I also felt between his words a deeper knowledge that perhaps Mary wouldn't have survived if I hadn't taken his horse.

In time darkness swept through the room. Mary turned on a small lamp on a nearby table and kept the fire going while I rested. After a while she removed my shoes and socks and pants and began stroking my legs. She had heated some oil on the stove and she rubbed this warmly into my legs as she sang. I closed my eyes and went back to my childhood. One summer I got lost when I wandered too far away from home, down to the bluffs near the river. When night fell I went into a cave to seek shelter. I tried to sleep there but I couldn't. There were too many noises around me, I could feel the presence of others. So I passed the night singing and telling myself stories. At dawn I followed the light out of the cave and worked my way back home. When I came to the door of the house I looked inside and saw my parents at the far end of the house sitting there. My mother held a child on her lap—a newborn. Their faces held all the light of the sun over their backs, and there was laughter and singing. So I turned from the door and went back out under a big white pine to sleep. As I slept I dreamed I was between two people walking up a hill, holding their hands. When we reached the crest of the hill we heard a voice and stopped and turned. There at the bottom of the hill was a child singing. He sang so beautifully and simply that I felt his voice enter me and carry me back down the hill to where he was. Then I was the boy alone at the bottom of the hill singing for another to come back.

When I opened my eyes I saw Mary Squandum on top of me, her tears reflecting fire in the open door of the wood stove streaming down her face. Through her passion, at that moment I felt every part of myself again. My legs came back to me.

GEESHIS

I know that when you leave a place and return again
the place changes, but when I went back to find
Franklin Sqaundum, to see the horse one last time,
I was not ready for such a change. Scavengers had
flown down and circled around the body of the dead
horse that I had cared for so much on the outside,
and what was inside of the animal was still steaming
with cold and warm, meeting in the same place at the
same time.

The car Franklin Squandum died in had shifted,
sunken further into the marsh up to the middle of the
windows. From where I stopped my car I could not
see him, so I walked out a ways toward the marsh,
around by the horse, and looked in through the
cracked web of glass that broke out from where
Squandum's heavy dark head had struck on impact.
Some water had sifted up inside the car, engulfing
part of his massive dead form, so he was part in
water and part out of water, at an angle covering part
of his face to the point where only an eye and a corner of the mouth were in sight in the fading sun. As
a pair of muskrats wiggled out from beneath the dash
and dove down to invisibility in a darker depth of
marsh, that one open eye gazed out into the twilight,
still specked with a semblance of light that I believed
let it see on after death, until the light cast further
into belief of the death of a man who used the light
to make the mind see whatever it was Squandum
saw in his lighted world.

I went back to the horse then and touched the head and looked into the eyes of the animal one last time, where I saw for the last time the first star in the red sky, just as I'd seen the same first star for the first time years ago when I put my hand out to the first red horse I'd been given as a boy. This time, however, I did not get on the horse's back and ride off to the village to see the woman I was to marry; this time I put tobacco down and got in my car and drove to town to tell the sheriff about a dead man in a sinking car on the road to Megis Lake.

FRANKLIN SQUANDUM'S DEATH DREAM
A MINI-DRAMA FOR NATIVE DANCERS

Scene One

Scene: A background of trees, some white, some brown, some deep in shadow, some with luminous trunks, some with leaves flickering with light. Far off a river flows into a lake, which is but a spot of blue light on the background.

Enter a man in a suit and a tie on a white horse. He reins the horse as if to guide it on an unfamiliar trail. Enter a dancer, dancing in full powwow regalia from a position at the back of the stage.

Man: Whoa! *(The horse stops.)*

Dancer: Ho Wah! *(The dancer continues, circling the man and the horse.)*

Man: What are you doing here?

Dancer *(still dancing):* I'm dancing. See, I got a number and everything. It's a contest—grass dance.

Man: You can't dance here. I own this land. Who are you and what are you doing on my land?

Dancer: I told you. I'm a dancer and I'm dancing and I was dancing here a long time before you came. You're probably lost.

Man: Lost! I'll show you who's lost. I've got a deed right here in my pocket. *(He reaches into a breast pocket, extracts the deed quickly and holds it out to the dancer while leaning down from the horse.)*

(The dancer keeps dancing, circling the man a few times, until the man, tired of reaching, jumps off the horse and follows the dancer around, waving the deed out to him.)

Man: It says right here . . .

(Suddenly the dancer snatches the deed.)

Dancer: It says "nw 40 × sw 40 × w 40 × e 40." This deed don't say nothing about this land. Chicago Title, is that you? I thought you said this was your land.

Man: Of course it's not me; it's my company—my father's company . . .

Dancer: Your father. Well, where's he at?—I thought you said this was your land.

Man: He's at home in Winnetka . . .

Dancer: Winnetka—sounds Indian. I thought you said this was his land or your land.

Man: That's correct.

Dancer: Well, if his home's in Winnetka, how could this be his land? He doesn't even live here.

Man: He bought it, years ago, if you'll examine the deed.

Dancer: From who?

Man: From the state, I think, or maybe it was part of an estate. I'm not sure, but I'm here to look the place over. We are going to build a resort complex. This land is perfect; it runs all the way to the river clear over to the lake.

Dancer: It goes a lot further than that. Where'd the state or the estate get the land?

Man: I'm not here to argue—I'm a developer. I'd suggest you leave.

Dancer: Suggest what you want. I can't stop dancing until the drum and the singers quit, and they been going a long time.

Man: I don't want to have to call the authorities.

Dancer: Who?

Man: Whomever . . . the County Sheriff, the State Police, if need be.

Dancer: What do they know about this?

Man (*getting back on his horse, grabbing the deed*):   I have the deed.

Dancer: Are you sure you aren't lost?

Man: Of course I'm sure.

Dancer: Look around. Does anything look familiar to you? Do you see anything in this place you recognize?

Man: I see surveyors' flags. I see potential. I see a corner quick mart, a place where tourists can buy gas, fill huge Styrofoam containers with cool green liquid. A place where children can find a candy bar, where worried mothers can buy aspirin, nonaspirin for feverish kids. A place where short-sighted vacationers can locate matches, paper towels, toilet paper. I see more: the whole lakeshore lined with cottages, a golf course inland, tennis courts. Simple pleasures born of the fruits of years of labor, here in paradise. I'll call it . . . Rainbow's End . . . the Land of the Holy Mackerel . . . Columbus's Garden. This land has potential.

Dancer: You're lost.

Man: I am not lost! This is my land. I own it; my father bought it. I'm calling the authorities. (*He pulls a cordless phone out of the horse's saddlebag, starts punching numbers as drumming wells up in the distance and grows louder and louder, almost deafening. Into phone*) I'm sorry . . . what did you say? No, listen. (*Screaming now*) The police . . . I said the police. (*The man turns the horse and rides off screaming into the phone. The dancer goes on dancing.*)

Interlude
Forty-nine scene—drumming and singing—the stage gives way to drummers and singers.

Forty-nine number one

So the shadows grow between us
so the shadows grow
I won't tell my best friend
if you come with me we'll go
up to a lonely hill
down to some secret place
maybe in the morning
I'll remember your sweet face
away hey yey yey hey yey hey
away hey yey yey hey
I'll remember your sweet face.

Forty-nine number two

On snakes from the great swamp
birds from sky and sun
An Anishinabe woman made me do things
I shouldn't have done
ya way ya ya hey ya ya
ya way ha ya hey ta ta she said hey ta ta
with honey on her lips
and fry bread in her lodge
when her Galaxy turned over
I took her in my Dodge
ya way ya ya hey ya ya
ya way ha ya hey ta ta
she said hey ta ta with lard inside her belly
and mahnohmin between her teeth
she made me share my blanket
then filled me up with grief
ya way ya ya hey ya ya ya way ha ya hey ta ta
she said hey ta ta
I gotta go

You know my whatacall's gonna be here
with his whatacall attitude
I gotta go
she said hey ta ta.

Forty-nine number three

(Oh is it?)

Hey yey yey hey yey yey
everytime I tell you the way
you say nah nah nah
hey yey yey yey
Oh is it?

Hey yey yey hey yey yey
everytime I explain myself
you say yay yay yay
hey yey yey yey
Oh is it?

Hey yey yey hey yey yey
when you mean really?
you say yay yay yay
hey yey yey yey
Oh is it?

Hey yey yey hey yey yey
when you mean I hear you
you say yay yay yay
hey yey yey yey
Oh is it?

Forty-nine number four

An all-night forty-nine
an all-month affair

then a couple of years in A.A. Aaaayyy
and a couple of kids somewhere.

A couple of couplings for a little while
a couple more for the road.
If I'd known you were doing to me
(to me) what I thought I was doing
    to you
(to you) I wouldn't have followed,
I wouldn't have followed you home.

Scene Two
Amid great laughter and continued singing, fading
into to songs in the background, a singer steps from
the shadow with a flute in his hand. He begins to
play, until the flute blends from the drum accompaniment to a single whistling voice in the dark. But as
the flute song continues, light shines forth beginning
a new day. A young man steps out of the darkness
from the back of the stage and to the soft sounds of
the flute he speaks out.

Young Man: The sun has returned now. It has
given its report about those days that have preceded
this one. So once again a story sets out among us.
You will see the story and where it came from this
time, but at other times the story comes from another
direction, waking all those who sleep in its narrative
path. Maybe this is why you see when you wake that
others have risen before you, or that as you wake
others still are rising up to set out from the place
where vague and indistinct dreams have visited them
to move out from beneath thick blankets of stars and
gift cloth.

(The young man smudges the stage, then the stage lights move one at a time on separate individuals rising and dressing ceremoniously in powwow regalia and dream clothes. Dancers include all of the people who have been mentioned in the stories to this point. The flute dies out. A soft drumming begins and each person, from oldest to youngest, when fully dressed, moves slowly through an arboreal eastern door, from which bright beams of many colors of light shine, into a dance circle. The drum gathers force and power, and at the height of percussive volume, shadows move in from offstage and surround the dance circle. Full light reveals uniformed police, state troopers, county cops, and the man from Winnetka with the deed. The head policeman calls out.)

Head cop: May I have your attention? May I have your attention, please?

(The dancers continue as the drum continues. The head cop nods to another officer and receives a megaphone. He flicks a switch. The first sounds come through in powerful electronic buzzing.)

Head cop: Attention . . . Attention dancers. You can no longer dance here. I have with me the owner of this property.

(The dancers and drummers stop, frozen, with their heads turned toward the speaker.)

Head cop: You must leave immediately; this man has a deed. (*The cop reaches over to the man and takes the deed. He holds it high above his head as he speaks.*) You must vacate these premises immediately. If we have to we will arrest every one of you, but we would prefer that you leave now.

(One dancer, an old man, speaks out.)

Old Man: Can we have a minute? I'd like to speak with the people, these other dancers here.

(At that, the dancers convene in a small circle just in front of the eastern doorway. They whisper in Ojibway, laugh, and walk back to the places where they stopped dancing.)

Old Man *(nodding to the drum):*   Continue the story.

(The drummers start up again, at full volume; the dancers whirl around.)

Head cop *(screams into the megaphone as he signals to the other lawmen with a wave of his hand):*   You are all under arrest!

(The officers break into the circle, grabbing dancers, scuffling as the singers continue. The head cop continues screaming and waving the deed as he works his way into the melee. Then, as he holds the deed above his head, a fancy dancer deftly snatches it from the head cop's hand and whirls away from the cop through a confusing mass of struggling cops and Indians. The dancer goes high and low and high, moving away from the red-faced cop. In time, after a few revolutions around the circle, the fancy dancer reaches down and puts the deed in the hand of a little boy, who dances, hiding the deed behind a feather fan. When the cop discovers that the fancy dancer no longer has the deed, he looks around the circle in confusion and in this way his movement, his confusion, makes him a dancer in time with the beat of the drum. In the meantime, the little boy gradually dances to the eastern edge of the circle, where the man from Winnetka catches a glimpse of the deed in the boy's hand. The man tries to run through the crowd to catch the boy, but his way is blocked by dancers and policemen still struggling in the circle. The boy then runs to the eastern doorway and arrives there just ahead of the man from Winnetka. Seeing that he will be caught, the boy climbs an eastern tree, a luminous white birch, with the deed in his hand. He climbs quickly, in contrast to the developer, who struggles with the tree by breaking branches and sliding back to the earth at almost every level. Soon the boy is at the top of the tree, where he finds a huge nest. He climbs into the nest as the man from Winnetka shouts in the dance circle to the head cop, who is locked in a fierce wrestling match with an Anishinabe woman.)

Man *(screaming):*   It's up there, in the tree!

Head cop: What's up there?

Man: The deed! The deed! A boy has it. He's in the nest, up there in the tree.

Head cop *(looks up to the tree as the woman jumps on his back):*   Where? I don't see a nest. What boy? *(He dances around in a circle with the woman on his back.)*

Man: The boy is in the nest, hiding. I saw him climb in with the deed. Do something. Stop this nonsense.

(The head cop pulls a pistol from his holster and fires into the air as he throws the woman from his back. The gunshot stops everything. The other lawmen draw their pistols and back slowly out of the circle, until all the dancers and singers are surrounded by armed lawmen.
A singer whispers under his breath to another.)

Singer #1: Looks like Wounded Knee . . .

Singer #2: Which one?

Head cop (*barks out in the direction of the singers*):
Quiet! This is gonna stop here and now. Don't anyone move. (*Looks at the developer.*) Show me where the deed is.

(They both walk over to the tree and stand, looking up.)

Man: Up there, see that nest at the top? The boy with the deed is in the nest.

Head cop: Where's my megaphone? I want to make sure this boy hears me. (*Another officer picks up the megaphone in the dance circle and brings it to the head cop.*)

Head cop (*into the megaphone*): Boy, this is state police officer King. I have the authority to arrest you and your folks right now. Drop the deed and come out of the nest and we will not press charges against you or your people. If you refuse, we will do whatever is necessary to procure the deed from you. Do you understand me, boy?

(Silence)

Head cop: Boy, come out now or send down the deed. *(Calls over another state trooper and whispers.)* Mullen, let's put a little scare into the boy. Fire a couple of shots up that way; that'll bring him out.

(Officer Mullen draws his gun from his holster and aims up towards the nest, but as he gets ready to fire, the fancy dancer screams out and rushes toward trooper Mullen. He tackles the officer just as he pulls the trigger and a bullet fires up through the tree, piercing the nest, snapping a few twigs forming the nest. The boy yells out from inside the nest. The gun goes off again as the men struggle on the ground, and the dancer goes limp, wounded in the chest.)

Head cop *(to another officer):*   Get help on the radio. Tell them two people have been hit out here. *(To the Indians)* Get this man a blanket. *(Four women rush to the fancy dancer and lay him on a star quilt.)* Someone else get me a chain saw. That boy sounded like he may have been hit; we've got to get him down.

(The scene fades to black.)

Scene Three
The stage fills with mist. The boy awakens; bone whistles well up in the distance. He is on the ground. The nest is on the ground upside-down, behind him.

He rises and moves vaguely around the stage, wandering alone, wondering where he is and how he arrived at this place. He remembers the dance and the deed. He goes back to the nest and looks around, walking around the nest, confused. He lifts the nest and crawls under.

Boy: This is not the same nest. There is a door. There was no door before.

(He sticks his head out of the door. Light shines through the mist from the east. Eagle dancers whirl out onto the stage, one after another. The boy watches. He hears crying and keening in the distance. The eagle dancers circle the nest and come before the boy, where they dance in place, slowly stroking their wings. The oldest of the eagles—a white eagle—speaks.)

White Eagle: You are in the doorway. You are wounded, but you will not die. You are in the doorway. Come out if you wish. On this side the councils are not always secret. Come out and follow the dance.

(The boy rises and follows the movement of the eagle. In a moment their forms are obliterated by intense bright stage lights. Then the boy is on the other side of a bright silver river, in a circle among men and women. The people are luminous, old projections, against the backdrop.)

Grandfather Beshig: This is the place of ancestors. (Points to the back of the stage, where pictures of Anishi-

nabe ancestors are projected on the back of the wall holographically, whole and in parts.)

Grandmother Neezh: Return what you have taken back to the earth.

Grandfather Nissway: We will give something to replace the paper, something you can hold when the men come to get you.

Grandmother Neewin: Think and pray when you are inside the nest. When it has fallen from the tree, rest there inside for a moment. Think and pray. You will fall near another tree. Put the paper in a hole beneath the tree at the place where an animal has dug. It will be there when you fall. Cover the hole with leaves. Then when the men have gone, bury the paper again in another place, in the lot near the cemetery at Four Bears. There we will give you something to replace the paper.

Grandfather Beshig: Go back now. Return to the doorway.

(The eagle dancers lead the boy away. On the way back he passes Franklin Squandum, the fancy dancer who was shot in the scuffle. Scene fades to black.)

Scene Four
The stage is as before. Policemen and dancers mill about. A few Indians haul away the dead dancer as women weep at his side. The drummers sing softly— a death song. The tree the boy was in has fallen. The nest has landed, upside down, very close to another

tree. Four officers lift the nest simultaneously. The boy lies inside, not moving. One of the officers pokes at him, another checks his pulse.

Officer #2:   He's alive and there's no blood. Wait, here on the arm he's been hit.

(The boy lifts his head and speaks groggily, as the old dancer comes to look him over.)

Boy: Grandfather? Where am I then?

Old Dancer: At the dance ground, Oskinaway. You were in the tree.

(The developer breaks in, searching around, scanning the ground near and around the boy.)

Man: What about the deed? What about the deed? What did you do with the piece of paper? Answer me.

Old Woman Dancer: Leave the boy alone. He has no deed. Can't you see he's been shot? There's no deed here. Go on back to your people. You're mistaken about this.

Head cop: The old woman's right. There's no deed around here. You must've seen things the wrong way.

Man: I saw the boy with the paper. I know I did. I demand justice.

Head cop: After we get things settled here, we'll go back and find your deed. But enough's enough for this day. This boy don't have the deed. Maybe he never had it. The last one I saw with it was that dead dancer. Have a little respect, man.

(With that the head cop leads the developer away. All the while the developer goes on and on.)

Man: I know I saw him with the deed. Check the nest again. I'll talk to the governor's office if I don't get some action soon. You better move on this . . .

(The stage fades to black and gradually lightens again. The drum sings an honor song for the dancer, as the stage lights focus separately on each of the dancers ritually removing their regalia. When the honor song is over the flute begins again and the young narrator returns.)

Young Man: Do not assume that what issues with the advent and cessation of human breath will remain visible, or will be untreated in the invisible places of thought. The exiled and the hidden know their own forms and their own survival even as they work through different seemingly apparent forms. If, for instance, a dancer falls where a tree has fallen, the acts we've witnessed are not limited to what we see or hear. The sun will give a report, you know, and the report includes all that in light and darkness we remember and never saw.

(The flute goes on . . . The stage fades to black.)

SQUANDUM'S FUNERAL

One reservation road runs to where the sun begins at this time of year, until it veers back north, around Megis Lake through the wildlife refuge to the center of tribal operations some ways south. Going the other way the road runs into the sundown center at this time of year and passes through Four Bears village, past where a housing project sprouted out just after the treaty payments came and went in the early 1960s. Between the rising and setting sun another road runs from the main street of the town of Tamarack to a T where the big white Catholic church rests as the largest, tallest landmark between the two settlements. The cemetery where Sqaundum will go into earth lies right next to the church on the eastern side, one hill away from the river.

For three nights the guildhall lights have blared out onto the road carrying the singing of the old people, taking in the shadows of those who have come through the night to sit through the night to see the clear passage of Squandum's huge physical shape into the spirit world. The old women have prepared feeds, the old men have spoken of the boy, of the man, of the shape and substance of the life of this Squandum with the knowledge that what he will see in his passage is beyond his own crossing and articulated in the songs they will sing him to help him pass over.

In the morning, it is done. The wake is over and four singers rise in the clear dawn from the east and

gather at Four Bears. At the request of the Squandum
family the singers take out the dream drum and walk
to the highest hill overlooking the village, a solid
echo away from the church. There the drum is established in its place and Seed withdraws a pipe. After
offering tobacco, after smoking in silence, Seed
returns the pipe, hands each drummer a stick, and
begins to tap lightly on the skin of the drum face.
It is here on the drum that Seed sees other villages
painted in circles around the edge of the drum,
painted at the bottom among greenery and earth
blossom splendor, painted at the top in a blue
ephemeral sidereal world. Between villages, faces
both human and animal vibrate at the door of each
lodge, with each striking of the singers' synchronous
sticks, as does the full form of the image of the great
bird overseeing the story on the drum.

At the same time four men dig Squandum's grave.
Nodin is deep in the hole, pressing into the earth as
the others stand up above him smoking and talking.
One after another they finish their smokes and drop
the burning ashes into the hole. Each in turn digs a
little deeper into the earth, remembering and digging
for Squandum.

Seed's voice sets out first, emitting mists and gathering volume as every other singer joins in. At some
point in morning red light, the articulated mists and
voices merge, gliding toward the river, flowing into
the last of an even larger fog, covering only the river
face. As the sticks strike against one village, people in
Four Bears wake and begin preparations for Squandum's funeral.

In time even the river mist fades and the singer's
voices give way to the voice of the huge iron bell in

the church tower. Squandum lies in an open casket in the center aisle of the church, just in front of the opening in the communion railing. Behind him a thick golden Bible lies open atop an altar made of birch logs. Off to the right, a young boy lights candles, as people file in from the back of the church. An old woman works her way up the aisle and stops at the side of the casket. She gazes deeply, intensely at Squandum, for a long time. Two children wander up behind her and peer over the edge of the coffin. Their eyes try to find what the old woman sees for so long, so deeply. When the old woman goes, Squandum's mother stands from her seat at the front of the chapel. Through tears she takes in the image of the man again, she touches the man again.

The priest enters from a doorway to the left beyond the altar, beside the big golden cross, at the back center of the chapel. His vestments flow over his body, swishing as he walks into the sound of a Christian hymn, sung in Ojibway. Beaded woodland patterns run the length of the stole draped over his robes into full blooming Anishinabe flowers up around his shoulders.

He opens the funeral mass with a calm exacting voice. In time this voice becomes a thin echo in a hall of dreaming heads. Relatives dream back to the boy Squandum, stepping onto a bus, uniformed and headed for war. Children dream of an open church door, letting them out into the sunlight, where they can run one another down for some particular teasing. The old people dream of this road to the church, of every house on the road, of every child born in every house, of every child gone to the cemetery before them. Then the dream becomes remembrance as the priest steps down from the step to the altar and descends into the center aisle swinging a censer in slow, pendular arcs, in dreamtime emissions of smoke, of incense fragrance sensed, fragrance gone. After the priest hands the censer to the altar boy, as he makes his way to the front of the church to begin a benediction, a deer bursts in from the back of the church, wanders, hooves clacking, up the center aisle, and looks into Squandum's casket. The priest is dumbfounded, his arms open, his palms suspended skyward like a man feeling for rain in full sun, with no words or prayer for a common gesture. The rest of the church is supended as well, though in deeper breaths and more confused thoughts. A child in the back whispers out, "Bell," another child giggles. Then with the first spoken word of the priest, the deer recklessly runs out the back door of the church. The priest closes the lid on Squandum's casket, and the procession to the cemetery begins.

The Deer Story
Brother found the deer in the refuge. He'd gone out hunting there and he said he saw this baby deer, alone, wounded, trapped under a fallen tree. (I believe he shot the mother.) He brought the deer home in the car. I heard him pull up, and I looked out through the screen door to see what he had. When he opened the back door of the car the deer jumped out and bolted around the house to the shed. I ran out right then and followed brother as he followed the deer. I don't know what happened next, but I saw brother then standing out-side of the shed by our house looking in through the door of the shed. The deer was inside there. I went right in and started talking to the deer, like I do to my dogs and the other animals I know. The deer listened and I told brother to go

get some food, an apple or some corn. After some time, the deer trusted me. I fed it and talked to it. I raised the deer from that day on. In time I even got it to drink milk from a bottle, like a baby. That deer even slept with me when it was younger. Pretty soon word got around and some people from the newspapers came out and took a picture of me under a table hugging the deer. In time the deer was like one of the family. It even had a mean, mischievous, streak, like my brothers and sisters. Sometimes it got me into trouble with the old women of the village. The deer liked to jump out at the old women and bump them as they went by our house on their way to church on Sundays. After the deer knocked old lady Shonyah into a ditch, all the women in our village carried sticks when they walked by our house. A few even threatened to have someone kill the deer. I put a bell around the deer's neck then, as a warning to the old women and so nobody would shoot it during hunting season. Then everyone started calling the deer Bell. As the deer got older it would wander off sometimes at night, and in the silence of the village you could make out where it was by the bell. Once it went out and was gone for a couple of days, and when it came back the bell was gone. I didn't see or hear that bell again until brother came back from the war drunk one night, laughing and hollering. One of his girlfriends was wearing that bell, like a necklace, shaking everyone awake and laughing.

At the grave site, Nodin aims at the sky in a salute to Squandum. As he squeezes the trigger he grimaces and catches the sun flash on gunmetal. Then he and Squandum are together again, in Vietnam, stoned on a hillside. "Keep shooting," Squandum screams. "They're over there in the trees, dancing, mocking us. Keep shooting." Squandum keeps shooting at the trees swaying in the humid wind. The whole company is shooting at what Squandum sees. When they advance to the enemy position, Squandum sees shot-up trees. "We got em," he says. "We got 'em all."

Then Nodin brings the gun to his side and two old veterans move to gather the flag draped across Squandum's casket. As they hold the flag between them, the deer bursts out from the shadows of trees and races between the two veterans. The flag wraps around the swift deer and covers its head as it bounds away toward the river. Nodin and the other veterans follow after the deer. At the river's edge, they see the flag in the river, sinking, whirling away in the rapids.

At the cemetery, up beyond the hill, Squandum's body finally descends into the ground, as Nodin hands Squandum's mother another efficiently folded triangulated flag.

REQUIEM FOR A LEG

What seems to have vanished forever often reappears
at the strangest moments: sometimes among diora-
mas of stuffed buffalo, stalked by synthetic, spear-
wielding hunters covered with actual wolf skins,
sometimes among fictional river villages among
imaginative reconstructions of mound builders, cata-
logued in curio stasis, as if the vanished were never
meant to exist in a moment beyond the fictional situation, but were instead left to struggle with another
simulated reconstruction, as invisible victims of the
interpretation of artifact. So when Oshawa walked
into the natural history museum of a large midwest-
ern city, as a young man of an urban reservation, a
cultural-exchange project between a large university
and a small reservation village, his own curiosity
about the authentic leg preserved in dry ice crept up
on him and sent him drifting back upriver to his own
home, where he was sure he'd heard his uncle tell
him a story about such a leg.

Was this a common practice his uncle told him about?
Did every village have such a story about such a leg?

He looked closer, more intently, at every detail,
the moccasin design stitched into the animal hide,
the cloth covering of the leg, the floral pattern
woven into cloth, the brown flecks of tobacco,
still extant between the ice and the human part.
He looked at the plaque on the wall next to the leg:

An Ojibway leg, circa 1880–1940. Though it
is not known why the leg was left like this,

some scholars believe burying a leg in full
ceremonial legging was a common practice
in the reservation period.

Oshawa looked again and he remembered
everything.

When he went home that spring, he went straight
to his uncle's place. He found the old man there, still
and quiet, in a wooden chair, smoking under the
shadow of an oak. As he neared, he thought uncle's
eyes were far off, perhaps attempting to follow the
sounds his ears heard roads away or skyward among
a formation of geese. But as Oshawa drew closer he
heard that the old man was listening to himself and
seeing something else altogether, for he hummed
and sung softly an old country-and-western tune,
between wisps of smoke with his eyes squeezed
shut.

"Uncle," Oshawa said, "I remember a story you
told me once. It was the story of Four Bears and the
leg and the storm and the books and the library."

The old man opened his eyes. "Nobody knows
that story. I've never told it to anyone."

"Yes, once when you were drinking, after old man
Four Bears died."

"But the leg," the young man went on. "Do you
remember what the leg looked like?"

"I remember every detail of that whole day. I've
dreamt of that leg a hundred times, just as it was
when the old man's daughters dressed it."

"What about the daughters, and the son? Do they
remember? Could they recognize the leg?"

The old man closed his eyes again and hummed
out another tune, the tune he heard on the radio the

morning Sonny Four Bears came to get him. He saw himself crossing the road again; he saw the leg in the crotch of the tree.

"I've seen the leg too, uncle," Oshawa said.

The old man quit humming. He looked hard at his nephew. "Sometimes dreams travel that way," he said. "Don't be afraid. Put tobacco out if you have some kind of fear about it."

"No, in a museum. I saw the leg on the wall in a museum in Minneapolis when I was down there this fall. I think it was the same leg. It was hung up, preserved in dry ice, on display with pipes and villages from the past. I recognized the leg from the story."

"It couldn't be," the uncle said. "That happened too long ago. The cloth would be rotten; the flesh would be gone."

Then the old man closed his eyes again and he saw himself again, struggling against a big white wind. When he woke, the village had gone dark and Oshawa was gone.

Oshawanung worked his way up the road the next morning, bent over and ambling with his carved cane. He could tell by the tracks in the road that the young man had traveled the same road earlier, and he knew where Oshawa had gone. He was right: when the sun glare melted off the front window of Willow Four Bear's house he could make out the shapes of the young man and the woman, sitting across from each other, engaged in conversation. They saw him coming and both rose up from the chairs to greet him as he ascended the four wooden steps to enter the house. Willow went to the kitchen and poured him a cup of coffee. She handed the old man a white cup, then poured milk into it, and he circled the cup with two unsteady hands.

"I'm going to call Sonny," the woman said. "He can go over to the museum and see if that really is Father's leg. He'll remember."

The old man leaned back into the softness of his chair and held his eyes on a velvet painting of an eagle dropping feathers to the earth, as he spoke, "What if the leg *is* your father's leg? How will you get it back? How will you prove that the leg belonged to your father? Those people will fight you on this."

Willow answered, "Enough people know what the leg looked like, at least four who are still living. Between those people we should have enough grounds to have the leg returned and reburied, according to my father's original intentions. How could those people argue such a case? Some white man must have dug up the leg, somehow. I don't know, but I do know it is not right for those people to have that leg."

Oshawanung assented hollowly, narrowly refraining from forming further points of argument against the wishes of a Four Bears woman.

Sonny Four Bears didn't see the leg at first. Like the rest of his family he found himself woven from where he stood in the darkness into the reality of each lit display, marveling at the detail, of the artificial figures, imagining himself in such a world. It wasn't until he had entered an interactive village and peered into the simulated fire in a model wigwam that he heard his youngest daughter holler, "Hey, look at the leg."

When he reached the place where the leg hung

on the wall, he knew immediately that the leg was his father's leg. So he took out his camera and shot picture after picture of the frozen leg. He shot partial photos of the moccasin, the legging, the plaque next to the display. When he finished, he drove straight to a one-hour photo-developing store, ordered two copies of each shot, then waited, over a beer, in a pizza parlor with his family. Inside he knew he could not shrink from the truth, though he contemplated lying to his sisters and burning the pictures. Yet, at the same time, he knew then that someone else would see the leg under similar circumstances and the word would travel back to him and he would have to go through the whole mystery again. Or worse, he thought, someone who had no connection to the family, some aimless Indian politician with a bad blend of education and self-righteousness would view the leg as an issue not of family but of all Indian people across the whole uninvolved country.

So he mailed the photos out to Willow the next morning and waited by the phone each evening with a bottle of port and a box of crackers. When the phone rang three days later, Willow only confirmed what he knew already: the leg was absolutely his father's and she wanted it out of the museum, to be reburied.

In a short time, Willow garnered the support of the tribal council and the tribal attorney. The council passed a resolution and the attorney issued a letter to the museum. Museum officials responded civilly but curtly with, in essence, a series of statements that questioned the memory of the Four Bears family and asserted various theories on the nature of ownership.

A hearing on the ownership of Moses Four Bears'
leg began that summer in a sweltering federal courtroom in downtown Minneapolis. In light of the tribal
attorney's inexperience in matters other than gaming
laws and post–Reorganization Act politics, the tribe
and a few upper-middle-class advocates for Indian
rights procured an East Coast lawyer named Catullus
Cage, a high-priced radical known for fearless legal
circumambulations and avant-garde courtroom
antics. For their part, the museum employed an
Ottawa Vietnam veteran named Tony Nugush, who
had lost an arm to a human Viet Cong mine, graduated at the middle of his class at the University of
Michigan Law School, and then graduated to a practice in Washington, D.C., to a firm he never lost a
case for. The case was heard before Minerva Salazar,
a Hispanic judge recently appointed to the bench by
a Republican president who liked her record on
affirmative action.

Cage began the case with a request for an honor
song. He walked to the back of the courtroom and
dramatically placed a burgundy box of Velvet tobacco
into the open hand of the lead singer of the Red
Branch Singers, from the Minneapolis Indian Center.
The singers stood up, lifted a red blanket covering
the drum, and walked toward the front of the courtroom. The bailiff, Cage, and a few officers of the
court procured chairs for each of the four singers. At
this point, the lead singer lifted a box of Marlboros
out of his breast pocket and passed cigarettes around
to each member of the drum. The courtroom waited
while they smoked. Then, just after, the singers
began to tap the drum gently. As the lead singer

leaned over the drum, whispering vocables to the
other singers, Tony Nugush called out from his place
at the defense table, "Your Honor, may I approach
the bench?"

At Salazar's approval, Nugush and Cage both went
to the front of the courtroom and looked over the top
of the bench at the puzzled judge.

"This is highly inappropriate, your Honor. An
honor song, such as requested by Mr. Cage, has
no relevance to the case and no stated recipient of
honor. As an ex-dancer and singer, I find the use
of the drum is culturally inappropriate. We must not
turn this courtroom into a powwow, in the twentieth-
century sense, and we must not—"

Cage jumped in. "Your Honor, Mr. Nugush has
been in Washington too long; for him to presume that
there is no honoree for the honor song is unfair and
ill founded. The request I gave with the tobacco designated honoring the United States court system and
the viability of that system in the interpretation and
understanding of distinct, multivalent cultural systems. One honor song will impose no further cultural
intervention in the courtroom atmosphere, nor will it
directly bear on the outcome of this case—a case that,
I remind you, hinges on creating an atmosphere in
which Native witnesses will feel at home."

"Mr. Cage," the judge spoke sternly to the two
men, "Mr. Nugush, let me warn both of you that I
will not tolerate convoluted cultural banter in the
course of this case. Both of you are experienced
enough to know that I will decide this case on the
legal issues involved. Therefore, any starlit dreams
you have of affecting the outcome of this trial with

publicity-hunting courtroom antics are best left
where you found them, in your egocentric heads.
As for the honor song, I see no reason to deny one
song for honor."

When the two lawyers returned to their places, the
Red Branch singers sang. Then the hearing began.

The Opening Arguments

Catullus Cage: How does the truth come to us?
Does it recognize us from afar and run to catch up
to us on a well-traveled road? Does it see us across a
great wide river and cross over against a strong current of current thought to come to meet us? I'm sorry,
but I don't believe justice is relative. This is a courtroom, a place built in theory and fact from human
imagination and symbolic conceptualization of that
imagination. On the other hand, the courtroom as
place is peopled by living, breathing human beings
who just happen to be in the same human construct
under the same set of circumstances. It is a hot day in
August. We are witnessing a trial for the return of a
human leg. But we are not all sitting at the same place
in the same construct. Some of us are sitting up
toward the front of the courtroom, where most of the
dialogue and most of the action deciding this trial will
take place. Some of us are sitting in the audience,
outside the dialogue, outside the action. This differ-
ence in perspective may possibly affect our perception, reception, apprehension of the evidence presented to us in the course of the trial, but I believe the
truth will become clear to each and every person who
visits this courtroom during the tenure of this case,

because that is what this case is about, the apprehension of truth. In this case the apprehension of truth rests on understanding how something cut off from human existence comes to represent a mere object of limited human possibility. And in this case we will learn how perhaps possibilities for human existence are greater than the perceptions of the museum, the keepers of limited objects. We apprehend the truth as we become part of the story, and the story always brings the truth back to us in some form. In this case, the form is the leg of Moses Four Bears, deceased tribal elder. In this case, the form has come to this courtroom to reassert a misunderstanding, a misconception, a mishandling of some part of the story that is our past. And I believe that if we mishandle the story here, the story will gather more force, more power, and assert the truth at another distant point, in another place that is meant to represent the highest standards of human conduct. Imagine being a descendant of Four Bears. Imagine walking into a place that is created for the sole purpose of allowing people to take a shallow glimpse at the past. Imagine seeing in that place a part of your own human ancestry, hanging on the wall, dressed for a different journey. You don't have to imagine. The story of the leg will do it, and in so doing the story will allow each of us to walk away knowing the truth.

Tony Nugush: How ironic to speak of truth at a trial that involves a physical part of a human being that exists in the absence of thought on the part of that human being. Old man Four Bears is gone, and his mind is gone with him. Who, then, does this leg belong to, assuming that this leg once was attached to Four Bears? My clients and I are of the contention that there is no direct proof that the leg in question is the leg Moses Four Bears walked around with for sixty years. As for stories and truth, we all, every one of us, can imagine that a story is true, but the thought generating a story doesn't always convey the same relationships of images and symbols from the teller to the receiver. In this courtroom we should be beyond the once-upon-a-time stage. I think the truth of this case will become clear as well. The leg frozen in this box, kept up and maintained by the museum, exists as a leg by itself, as part of the holdings of the museum. This leg has no name, no face to go with it. The museum set the leg up to illustrate an aspect of human existence; this is how a leg looks, this is how an actual leg was dressed in an actual community, at an actual place in an actual time. This is how people become educated about other people who live and work in the same cultural milieu. Yes, we can learn from the past. We can all learn by seeing the leg of a person preserved for us, to present each and every one of us with the truth, not in a story but in a real-life preserved human image. Moreover, this case should not, must not, be decided on cultural mean-derings of individual memory, but on legal issues of ownership, on evidence, on the laws of the nation under which this courtroom serves. I believe the evi-dence, devoid of empathy for what has been lost or misplaced by the well-intentioned Four Bears family, will show that the leg in question belongs to the museum and the people who have preserved the leg for all these years.

Witness No.1

Cage: Your Honor, I'd like to call the first witness, Willow Four Bears.

(Willow stands from her place next to Cage at the prosecution table. When she arrives at the front of the court near the witness box, the bailiff waits with a Bible.)

Cage: Ms. Four Bears, would you feel better with some other item to swear on?

Willow: No, the Bible is fine. I'm Indian, but I go to church too.

(The bailiff holds out the Bible, raises his right hand to eye level, and guides Willow Four Bears through the swearing-in. Then the old woman seats herself in the witness box behind a microphone.)

Cage: Tell me, Ms. Four Bears, about your father. What it was like growing up as you did?

Willow: My father, Moses Four Bears, was a great man, well respected throughout our village and beyond. He brought our family through hard times on the reservation, through those years when things were changing on the reservation. He was a good man, honest, and he had a big heart. He wouldn't let people go without; if families needed help, he'd help provide. When he came back from a hunt with food, he'd share with elderly people of the village. That's the way he was. He always treated my mother well, and he taught us to be respectful. He also taught us to be strong through hard times. There was a deep faith in my father that I carry with me to this day.

Cage: Were you close to your father?

Willow: He didn't always show how he felt about us, but we knew by what he did for us that he cared for us. My father has always been close to my heart.

Cage: What do you remember about the day your father lost his leg?

Willow: Mother came into the room where my sister and I slept, early, before sunrise. "Get up," she said. "Your father needs us, now." Sister and I both woke and went out to the main room, where father lay on the sofa, sleeping. When I came into the room I noticed, right away, part of his leg was gone. Then my mother sent my brother, Sonny, over to Oshawanung's place to help out. She said Father wanted someone from over there to bury the leg for us. While Sonny was gone, she woke Father and he told us to start preparing a ceremonial legging for the leg, which was resting on a chair in a box. When those boys returned from across the road, Sister and I took out the red legging and the moccasin, just as my father asked. Then we dressed the leg and put it back in the box, nailed a cover on it, and gave it to Oshawanung to bury.

Cage: Do you remember anything else about that time?

Willow: After we gave those boys the leg, I never saw it again. Father was in pain, but he went back to sleep and we spent the rest of the day caring for him.

Cage: Is it safe to say that since you dressed the leg for burial, you could remember the details of the items you put on the leg?

Willow: I remember them well. I made the moccasins, the moccasin he chose to bury his leg in. I brought the mate to that moccasin with me. After my father died my mother gave me the moccasin for the other foot. It's over there on that table.

(At this point Catullus Cage moves pointedly to a table of exhibits and lifts a beaded moccasin from the table. At the same time he lifts the leg, preserved in dry ice in a box, and holds the moccasin up next to the leg in the box.)

Cage: Your Honor, let the record show that the moccasin brought to the courtroom is a perfect match, in every detail, to the moccasin on the foot of the leg from the natural history museum. *(Cage sets the moccasin down and holds the leg out in front of him to show Willow Four Bears.)* Can you definitely say that the leg frozen here, preserved in this box, is your father's leg?

Willow: Yes, I recognize the legging, the box, everything.

Cage: Thank you, Ms. Four Bears.

Judge Salazar: You may cross-examine the witness if you like, Mr. Nugush.

(Nugush stands and slowly moves to the front of the courtroom toward the witness box.)

Nugush: Ms. Four Bears, thank you for being here. Thank you for bringing yourself to this place to help us clear up this case. If you don't mind, I'd like to ask a few questions. Please think carefully before you respond. I wouldn't want you to misspeak or be misinterpreted. Do you know how your father lost his leg?

Willow: He had diabetes. They cut the leg off at the reservation hospital and then brought him home.

Nugush: According to the reservation hospital report, your father's leg was frozen. A tribal social worker found him in a ditch, passed out.

Willow: I was told he had diabetes. This is what my mother told me. That is what caused his death four years later.

Nugush: The report also said that Moses Four Bears was drunk at the time he came into the hospital.

Cage *(Rises violently from his chair):*   Objection! Whether Moses Four Bears was drunk or not has no bearing on the evidence the witness has given identifying the leg as her father's.

Nugush: Willow Four Bears was a young woman at the time her father lost his leg. The details of her testimony identifying her father's leg must be couched in her ability to remember and verify circumstances surrounding the removal of her father's leg. I'm attempting to show that Mrs. Four Bears may be refusing to acknowledge certain circumstances about how and why her father's leg was removed. These details may in fact relate to her reliability as a witness.

Willow: I've heard it said that my father had been drinking, but I was told by my mother that they removed his leg at the hospital because he had diabetes.

Nugush: As for the moccasin, you said you made it for your father?

Willow: Yes.

Nugush: When did you make it?

Willow: I made that moccasin two years before his leg came off, for a ceremony.

Nugush: What ceremony was that?

Willow: It was a ceremony to honor him for his service to people of our village.

Nugush (Walking over to the exhibit table, picks up the moccasin):   Tell me, are the designs on this moccasin, the red flowers, the green stems, are these unique designs among your people?

Willow: Not really; many women from our village make such designs.

Nugush: Well, is there anything in the threading, in the stitch, that signifies the handiwork of a particular individual? I mean, if I were to see another moccasin made by you, alongside this moccasin, could I somehow tell that you made it?

Willow: I don't know. I didn't sign my name in small beaded letters, if that's what you mean. But you must know that all things created have a certain signature, no matter how similar they must seem. I've hear it said, about some things like moccasins, that the signature is in the mistakes of the maker, in imperfect work.

Nugush: No, that's not what I mean. Let me put it this way. Could someone else make such a moccasin and make it so that we couldn't tell who made it?

Willow: Maybe, but why would they?

Nugush: Or could someone make such a moccasin by looking at it and reproducing the pattern and stitch from a photograph?

Willow: Maybe, but I believe you can tell that these moccasins go together. The age of the leather and the exact color of the beads shows that.

Nugush: But you're saying that the stitching and design work could be replicated.

Willow: Maybe. I'm not sure anyone would do that, but I suppose they could, and why would we want the leg if it wasn't my father's?

Nugush: Oh, I know why someone might repro-duce such a thing, but . . . Let's move on. Why do you think your father chose a different moccasin to wear when he died and was buried later? Why didn't he choose the moccasin to match the moccasin that was buried with his amputated leg?

Willow: I can't say, but it may be that my mother made the choice for his burial.

Nugush: Do you think you could identify your father's leg if the moccasin and legging on the leg as you now see it were not there?

Willow: I don't know what you mean.

Nugush: I mean, could you identify your father's leg if the moccasin and legging were removed.

Willow: I don't know. I suppose I could.

Nugush: But at this point you're almost certain that the leg is your father's just because it happens to be covered with articles of clothing you recognize?

Willow: It's not just the clothing.

Nugush: Do you know for sure what happened to your father's leg after Arnold Oshawanung and your brother took it away? Did you see them bury the leg?

Willow: No, I didn't see them bury the leg.

Nugush: So it is possible that the clothing you claim to recognize could be covering another man's leg?

Willow: I don't see that as a possibility.

Nugush: I don't know, maybe Arnold Oshawa-nung never buried the leg, or maybe he stripped it of its clothing. Or maybe the museum staff put the articles you claim to recognize on another leg.

Willow: Maybe it's your leg there in the box.

Nugush *(to Salazar):*   I have no further questions, your Honor.

Witness No. 2

Cage: Your Honor, I'd like to call Arnold Oshawa-nung to the stand, please.

(Oshawnung stands at the sound of his name and moves forward from his seat, one row back from the prosecution table. Like Willow Four Bears, he takes his oath on the Bible. Once in place on the witness stand, Cage takes over.)

Cage: Arnold, tell the court a little about yourself.

Oshawanung: My name is Arnold Oshawanung. I've lived almost all my life on the Fineday Reserva-tion, up north. People who know me know that my word is good, that my memory is clear. I'm known throughout Four Bears village as a man who will tell the truth. So I'm here to help the Four Bears family get back something that no one should be able to take away, the right to know that their ancestors rest in peace. More than that, all the people of our tribe should be able to rest assured in knowing that one of our tribal people can be reconnected, in every way, with the ground that is his home.

Cage: Thank you, Mr. Oshawanung. As Willow Four Bears told us earlier, you were the one the family gave the leg to, to bury. Is that right?

Oshawanung: Like she said, Sonny came over and got me early that morning. As we crossed the road back over to the Four Bears' place, I could see that we were in for a storm, though I didn't know how soon and how fiercly that storm would strike. I remember everything, though. I saw old man Four Bears on the sofa; I saw the leg in a box on the chair. The old woman and the girls were making preparations for the old man. When the leg was dressed, after he said a prayer and made a tobacco offering, he gave me instructions. Then Willow nailed the lid on the leg box and I took the leg out to bury it.

Cage: You say the old man gave you instructions. What did he say?

Oshawanung: He told me to bury the leg near a big tree, down by the river. He said, "Say a prayer over the leg and offer tobacco after you put the leg in the hole, before you cover it up."

Cage: Did you do that?

Oshawanung: That's a long story. I tried to do what the old man said, but the storm came in quick and the ground was frozen. I went out with Sonny, but we could hardly see through the depth of snow and the fury of the wind. I sent the boy back home and went on ahead toward the river myself.

OSHAWANUNG'S STORY
WAKING IN THE LIBRARY

I don't know how long I'd been sleeping, and I couldn't remember where the book I'd started ended and where the dream I'd fallen into started. But as I woke, I knew the storm had subsided into a day of sunlight. And as I saw the sunlight branching into the broken library window and looked around the room I'd forgotten in my sleeping, I regathered the details. The inside of the library had cooled some; the fire in the wood stove had burned away the legless tables and the broken chairs I had fed into the mouth of the stove. Books too were gone, burned away in my own fear of being trapped by a storm—though one book still lay open partly burned, blackened and aged by the heat inside the stove. And my fear didn't seem too far-fetched, as I gathered in the effects of the storm's powerful blasts into the room. Where I'd burned books, the storm had chaotically ripped books down from shelves, undoing the order they were subject to, scattering titles of history among fiction, piling words of scientists onto words of saints and obscure poets, bringing some books down from the shelves for the first time since they came into that room.

Seeing this made me want to leave at once. So I picked up the book I'd been reading and went to the door, turned the glass knob and pushed easily, expecting the door to spring open. But the door would not move, and again I remembered the

storm, the depth of snow outside, and I knew the
door would never open that way. Instead, I left the
library the way I came in, through the window
behind the table I'd propped up to block the wind.
Once outside I returned to the tree on the hill overlooking the river. When I looked into the crotch of the
tree where I'd put Four Bears' leg, I was overcome by
the brightness of the sun, which rested, at that time
of day, in the same division of branches. I lifted
myself as before and reached to feel for the wooden
box with my hands, to pull the leg down. I felt nothing and from that point of height in the tree I could
see there was no leg; it was gone. I searched the area
for hours. I went to the river, seeking an answer
along the banks of the frozen stream; I combed the
underside of the trees in the area. There were no
clues to the location of the leg, and I gave up looking.

I never told anyone this part of the story before.
I felt shameful about my inability to fulfill the old
man's request, and I felt a sense of despair about los-
ing the leg. I wondered if the leg would return someday, and for a few days, for a few mornings right
after, I would wake up and walk back to the tree,
hoping the leg would somehow be in the place where
I'd left it, lodged in that tree. My despair grew whenever I saw anyone from the Four Bears family, and
my shame told me to avoid them, especially after
they thanked me for taking the old man's leg and
acting according to his and their wishes.

I never let go of the secret I carried for all these
years, but as far back as I can remember I wondered
if the secret would be revealed to others in a way that
I wouldn't understand. I thought somehow invisible
tracks would lead people to the leg and I would have

to explain the disappearance of something I didn't understand myself.

I dreamt of the leg a hundred times since the day of the storm. Sometimes I looked out into a magnificient dream of sunlight and old people laughing and children running into butterfly fields, and the leg would appear in a hole in the earth and rise up of its own volition from the earth and chase me away from the beauty and splendor of a young man's dreams. At other times the leg would talk to me, as a voice from inside a box. In one of these dreams the leg said, "Recite four Hail Marys and six Our Fathers, always tell the truth." I said the prayers, but the dreams never went away. When Moses Four Bears died I filled two nights with prayerful request, but the leg kept coming back.

Now I am an old man who has suffered from something no one else knew, who has suffered a lie by not speaking about it, and this has led me to a roomful of strangers, of strangers I once knew but who now know me as a stranger, as a keeper of a heavy secret, of strangers I never knew, but who now know as much about me as people I lived with and saw all my life. If anyone in this courtroom can see the need for the proper return and reburial of Moses Four Bears' leg, it is me. I would like to help bury that leg as the old man requested so long ago. Perhaps that will bury the dreams that have haunted me for all these years.

(Catullus Cage draws back from the witness and speaks out into a big silence.)

Cage: I have no further questions.

(The judge aimlessly gazes at Tony Nugush, who sits upright in his chair, leaning forward with both elbows on the table in front of him, staring intently at Oshawanung.)

Nugush: I have no questions, your Honor.

Salazar: You may step down, Mr. Oshawanung. Thank you for your testimony. Let us recess until tomorrow.

SYSTEMS AND WITNESSES
FOR THE MUSEUM

Witness No. 3

Nugush: Your Honor, on behalf of the museum, I'd like to call Adam Post, Curator of the Twin Cities Metropolitan Museum.

(In a few moments Post is sworn in. Nugush rises to question the gray-haired curator first.)

Nugush: Mr. Post, how long have you been in charge of the Twin Cities museum?

Post: For well over ten years now. I started in October of 1970.

Nugush: Could you briefly outline, for the court, the mission of the museum?

Post: Our museum functions to educate the public about natural history, including the history of the earth, and its wide variety of animal, mineral, plant, and human species. We try to perform that function with the best available artifacts and scientifically sanctioned reproductions of the earth's biological communities.

Nugush: What sort of reputation does your museum have with both the public and the museum communities in which you operate?

Post: Our museum has always been cited as a valuable public education tool. Throughout the year we work hand in hand with public and private educational institutions to bring a clearer understanding of natural history to their members. In addition, we serve a lay persons' public, if you will, by providing the general populace with an intellectual and educational outlet as well. At the same time, a number of other museums throughout the country have modeled their exhibits and displays on the Twin Cities museum's example. Curators, scientists, and anthropologists from various museums come to us throughout the year to examine our procedures, practices, and techniques for presenting natural history to the public. We also have staff and scholars of the highest order, providing us with guidance. I can safely say that our museum is everything a natural history museum should be.

Nugush: I have no further questions.

(Cage steps to the center of the courtroom, emitting a soft whistle of disbelief.)

Cage: Mr. Post, you've given us an excellent insider's review of the value of your museum, and you've provided the court with some insight on the service and quality of the Twin Cities museum, but on a few points you lost me. The first is in regard to the concept of "scientifically sanctioned practices." What does that mean?

Post: I was referring to practices and theories commonly accepted in the modern scientific community.

Cage: Yes, now I understand. So you're saying there are ways of doing things that are deemed appropriate in terms of presenting natural history in the commonly accepted academic ways.

Post: Yes, I believe that's correct.

Cage: And it is in accordance with such views that your museum and its esteemed staff of technicians and scholars make museum policy decisions?

Post: Of course there are other concerns, some financial, some philosophical, but in many respects that is correct.

Cage: What kind of scientific practice or theory sanctions the display of a human leg as an artifact for public consumption, and what might the public learn about natural history by seeing such a leg on display?

Post: Our museum attempts to display natural history cultures and subcultures in manners that reflect the best possible representations of those cultures. In the case of the Ojibwa leg, we felt that we had an artifact that was undeniably authentic and representative of Ojibwa people. The leg gave us the unusual opportunity to show a one-of-a-kind artifact, an actual leg, the leg of a person who existed at one time in an Ojibwa community. This was one case in which we displayed more than a model; in other words, the object was not a model, the model was an object.

Cage: You say that this was an opportunity. I'm sure it was, but you say it was an opportunity based on using something real. How do you, or how did your staff, your experts, know that this leg was an Ojibwa leg?

Post: We knew by where the leg was found and by the way the leg was adorned.

Cage: In both cases, then, your knowledge that the leg was Ojibwa had nothing to do with the leg itself. That is, couldn't you say then that the importance of the leg as a model object rested in its identity, which was determined by factors external to the human leg? You could show the Ojibwa adornment without the leg, but you couldn't show the leg—with any significance as a model—without the Ojibwa adornment. If you did, you might have to rely on additional scientific practices to determine the ethnography of the leg. Moreover, you could never present the leg in the cultural context in which it was found, with anything but dubious scientific accuracy. I mean, what would you do without the adornment? Reconstruct the site where the leg was found as proof that the leg was Ojibwa? Therefore, since the authentic natural history of the leg was determined by an unduplicatable cultural context—and an assumption that what you find in a culture resides in and represents the culture—and by significant codes of adornment, you don't need the human leg as part of a display. A model would have sufficed, don't you think?

Post: I don't believe you represented the importance of the leg as it existed in a point in time, as the primary consideration in your argument.

Cage: Forgive me, but I can't help feeling your museum misrepresented the issue. Your framing, your using the leg as a model, displays only a partial view of natural history. Most often that view typifies narrow conceptions of physical processes: display the physical world; gloss over, in short automated speeches and brochures and clear concise identification display plaques, dynamic imaginative natural history as a series of progressive stages of static models.

Post: What other choices do we have?

Cage: What of humanity, of imaginative inter-action between humans and their worlds? What of the meaning of the leg to the people who knew the person who walked, ran, and lost that leg? Has your science brought us to this? Where is your humanity?

Salazar: Enough, Mr. Cage.

Cage: I have no further questions, your Honor.

Witness No. 4

Nugush: Your Honor, I'd like to call Professor Cody Williams to the stand.

(When Williams settles into the witness box, Nugush begins.)

Nugush: Tell us about yourself, your background, your professional life.

Williams: Yes. I am a professor at Brigham Young University, a doctor of anthropology. I did my undergraduate course work in anthropology at the University of Iowa, and I completed my graduate studies at the University of Minnesota. I've published four books on American Indian culture groups, and I've served as a consultant, an advisor, and a researcher for numerous museums, including the Twin Cities Metropolitan Museum. I'm currently the editor of the *Journal of Anthropological Studies*.

Nugush: You must be well respected in your field.

Williams: I believe so.

Nugush: Are you also well respected in the Indian communities you've written about?

Williams: Again, I believe I am. Throughout my career I've made every attempt to understand thoroughly the communities I've studied. In every case my study included extended prior research on, as well as extended residence in, the Indian communities. Time and again, representatives of these communities have commended me on my presentation of their culture. I have letters from tribal people that offer some proof of my competence and acceptance in working with Native American groups. Often those letters address intangibles: my consideration for cultural idiosyncrasies, my understanding of cultural practices in the way I approached people, in the way I worked with people, in the appropriate way I conducted myself in the community.

Nugush: Tell the court, if you will, Mr. Williams, how you came to discover the leg that is the subject of this court case.

THE ANTHRO'S TALE

At that time I was a graduate student gathering information for my doctoral dissertation. After some general preliminary research, I decided to do my dissertation on the Ojibwa as a river culture, as a people who interacted with river cultures. To gather research close to the source I went to northern Minnesota, to a small village on the Yellowhead River. When I got there, I intended to do everything the right way. I set up an Ojibwa lodge in the manner that my preliminary research suggested. I made my journey and set up camp just as the last days of winter faded into spring signs. I chose a spot across the river from the Four Bears village, yet in the general proximity of the same kind of river culture the village would experience in day-to-day life. This was the second phase of my research studies and the first phase of my fieldwork.

I had planned in the third phase—in the second phase of my fieldwork—to interview members of the Four Bears community and to work and live with them every day for a year. During that time I hoped to gather extensive notes, photographs, taped interviews, and cultural artifacts.

Those were my plans, but after about two weeks of living on the river in my wigwam, I made a significant discovery. As I went out one morning to catch some fish, a large piece of ice rolled over to where I had set up on the riverbank. In almost dreamlike fashion the ice turned a bend in the river and wound

its way to the relatively placid bend I fished from. As
the ice came nearer I saw something inside the ice or
beneath the surface of the river. As cold as it was, I
stepped off the bank into the water and wrestled with
the ice and dragged it, and the box beneath it, up the
bank. Then I immediately returned to my wigwam,
where I started a fire until I could melt the ice enough
to extract the wooden box. When I did I could tell the
inside of the box was frozen solid as well—perhaps
some water had seeped in and frozen the contents.
Of course the next step included opening the box. I
took a hammer and file and a few other tools and
pried the box open. Inside I found the leg, still
dressed, in almost perfect condition. Though I had
no idea about the significance, the meaning of the
leg, I knew that I wanted to preserve it as it was,
as a unique artifact.

I put the lid back on and I walked with the leg,
from my wigwam, back to the clearing at the side of
a two-track where I had parked my car, a mile or so
away from the field site. From there I drove to a place
called Strawberry's Bar, where I made a phone call to
the head of my dissertation committee. He told me to
keep the leg frozen, to find a place where I could preserve it temporarily until more sophisticated techniques were available to me. I hung up the phone
and asked the owner of the bar, a Sean Strawberry, if
he had a freezer I could use for a few hours. He said
he had a freezer, but he didn't know if I could use
it, since the freezer was for business purposes only.
I offered him twenty-five dollars, and after a few
more minutes of haggling he agreed to let me use his
freezer. I brought the leg in, set it in the freezer, and
went to a larger town nearby, twenty miles or so from

the reservation, to buy a large cooler and some dry ice. Then I went back to Strawberry's, picked up the leg, and drove straight to Minneapolis, where I met Professor Scoffner at a restaurant near the university. After I showed him the leg, we went back to his office. He called the museum immediately.

That evening we brought the leg to a meeting with the curator and a few members of the museum advisory board. It was clear that everyone was ecstatic, so ecstatic that Professor Ripley opened a bottle of the finest brandy the museum had on hand to celebrate the find. After Ripley opened a second bottle, our discussion entailed questions, speculations about the significance of the leg. Professor Scoffner posited quite eloquently the importance of the discovery, and he also accurately placed the leg in the proper cultural context.

A bit of debate ensued, but the debate revolved around the issue of why the leg was put in a box, and not what tribe the leg was from. The moccasin, the beadwork, the legging, the area of discovery, clearly denoted the tribal identity of the leg; everyone was in agreement on that. Professor Ripley, of the museum, suggested that the leg was an emblem of warfare, that the person who'd lost the leg was a victim of torture, and that the torturers probably cut off human parts, limb by limb, and floated them down the river as a reminder to enemies.

Though I was just a graduate student, I pointed out the absence of logic in such a view with questions such as: how could the torturers be sure that the enemy would find the leg, and if that was the purpose of the torturers, wouldn't they make a little canoe or raft for the leg, to make sure the leg floated

far enough and became conspicuous enough to catch
the eye of the enemy, instead of enclosing the leg in a
box? I also asked whether the torturer would let one
good moccasin, one excellent moccasin, go down a
river when the moccasin was still functional, as part
of a pair the torturer could have for himself, or at
least give to a friend.

Ripley hotly countered both of my arguments, first
by saying a leg in an open canoe or on a raft would be
fair game for carrion feeders, and if there were no
moccasin to identify the leg, how would the enemy's
family know enough to mourn or fear the death of
a loved one? The moccasin served as a form of
identification.

Professor Scoffner ended that line of speculation by
citing all the anthropological evidence his head could
muster and saying, "No, it's a known fact the Ojibwa
and most of their enemies tortured with fire. Besides,
the box and the wood of the box point to a postwar
time period." Then Scoffner introduced his theory of
the leg as part of a ritual to test the manhood of warrior initiates.

Ripley jumped on Scoffner's speculation with both
feet from a high and lofty perch. "What? Cut off a
man's leg to test his worthiness as a warrior? What
good is a one-legged warrior?"

I sheepishly intercalated, in that rare and brief
intellectual space, a theory of woodland horses and
artifical birchbark legs held together by sinew and
spruce pitch, but Scoffner knew I was patronizing
him and he turned the argument in another
direction.

"Perhaps," he said, "this treatment of the leg
involves a ritual for getting rid of diseases in the com-

munity, a dream ritual in which the leg takes the diseases into the purifying waters of the river."

"No," Ripley pressed in, "the leg is given to the river to ensure good fishing." The argument continued this way for a good while before we all realized the leg and the reason it was in the box could not be explained by any expert in our small circle. Still, we understood the value of the leg, and in a few days the museum offered to buy the leg from me for one thousand dollars. Though I suspected the price might be low, I assented with the understanding that I would be given full credit for the discovery of the leg in all museum literature for time immemorial. Ironically, even though I tried to change the focus of my dissertation to deal with the origins and purpose of the leg, I never found any primary or secondary research to solve the cultural enigma of the lost leg. And I did my dissertation on another subject, another tribe altogether.

Nugush: It seems clear, Mr. Williams, that you and the other experts who viewed the leg never considered the possibility of the leg belonging to a living twentieth-century Ojibway.

Williams: No, I did not. As soon as I saw the leg, I thought of a leg from an Indian of the past. My conversations with Professors Scoffner and Ripley supported my assumptions.

Nugush: You've heard the testimony of a few members of the Four Bears community. How do you perceive what they've said?

Williams: Though each Native witness seems to believe what they say about the removal and relocation of the leg, a number of matters are left unresolved by their testimony. If the leg was in a tree, how did it get into the river? Are we to assume it flew to the river? As for the physical evidence of the matching moccasins, in the time I've spent among Native people I've seen a great many pairs of moccasins similar to the moccasin on the leg. The design is common. The stitching is common. The material is common, and if you look close enough you will probably see that Willow Four Bears' moccasin is a bit more discolored than the moccasin on the leg.

Nugush: Thank you, Mr. Williams. I have no further questions, your Honor.

Cage: Mr. Williams, you say you found no information about the leg in your research subsequent to the discovery of the leg. Did you ever go to the Four Bears community to ask people there?

Williams: No, I did not. I thought of such action briefly, but such a course seemed unwise to me. I mean, should I have gone door to door with the leg, carrying it around until someone identified it? I was an unknown in the community at the time. How strange it would seem, a non-Indian stranger walking around with a leg, which was wrapped in Ojibwa finery, approaching people out of the blue, asking questions. Besides, my most immediate analysis told me the leg was older, of a time prior to the lives of the people in the community. I really thought the leg might go back to the days of the ancestors of the

people living in the community. So what could
they possibly tell me, or what would they tell me?

Cage: Gee, I don't know. A leg floats to you out
of nowhere, and your first thought is that no one
around the village will know anything. Only a few
days before, you were going to write a whole book on
what you thought the people would tell you. I bet
you saw an opportunity in the leg, a chance to cap-
ture something unique, a one-of-a-kind find that
would forever connect your name with an authentic
artifact.

Williams: How dare you make such assumptions—

Cage: Forgive me for my assumptions, Mr. Williams. If the museum should return the leg for
reburial, perhaps the Four Bears' family and Mr.
Oshawanung can forgive you for yours. I have no
further questions, your Honor.

Judge Salazar: Thank you, Mr. Williams, Mr. Cage,
Mr. Nugush. Since we have heard all the witnesses,
the court will adjourn until tomorrow. At that time
we will hear closing arguments, then I'll render a
decision.

Closing Arguments

Cage: Your Honor, we have all heard from the witnesses most intimately connected with this case. In
the testimony of witnesses on both sides of the issue
it is clear that this leg should return to the land of its
ancestors, its carrier, its other human part. The testi-

mony of Willow Four Bears and Mr. Oshawanung tell
the story in clear detail, of the removal of the leg and
its disappearance. Moreover, Ms. Four Bears has
produced substantial physical evidence that shows a
link between her father and the leg. And it is not hard
to believe that the leg might have somehow fallen
from the tree Oshawanung placed it in, and slid
down the riverbank into the river, upstream from
where Cody Williams found the leg the following
spring. In fact, the sequence of events, the seasonal
change from winter to spring, may have precipitated
melting on the river and that, of course, moved the
leg in the direction of the esteemed anthropologist,
Mr. Williams. Beyond the sequence of events, I
must also question the motives of the museum in
wanting to keep this leg on display. By all accounts
the museum is unsure about the cultural context
in which the leg belongs, and therefore their own
tenets for displaying the leg in any cultural context
are imperfect and outside the reason for which the
museum exists—at least according to the testimony.
I have no choice but to conclude that what the
museum fears most has come to pass in this trial.
Their use of Moses Four Bears' leg shows arbitrary
judgment, pious self-righteousness framed in the
interest of research, an understanding of natural
history and language that affords certain seers the
option of not seeing how their views affect the seen.
As a famous philosopher once said, "The beginning
is the result." As soon as Cody Williams picked up
Moses Four Bears' leg, he left the story unfinished in
every scientific detail. He could not determine the
source, the time period, or the significance of the leg
in accordance with the standards with which he and

his peers so closely identify. Of course, this is just part of the story. The deeper, more cumbersome story rests in five hundred years of human history on this continent, in the arbitrary manner in which Eurocentric intellectual culture mongers and mythmakers have judged the first inhabitants of this land. They've killed them, set plagues upon them, and then after they are dead, these same people, or at least their descendants, want to remove the remains of the dead and study them, catalogue them, and display them. Returning Moses Four Bears' leg to his homeland, according to the wishes and the judgment of his family, may seem like a small part of that larger story, but such a return would be only proper and just, given the evidence at hand. Thank you, your Honor.

Nugush: Mr. Cage has spoken very dramatically on the victimization of Native peoples across the land, yet victimizing the purported victimizer in no way provides a firm foundation for deciding the legal issue of this case. Who does the leg belong to? Even if the court accepts the view that the testimony absolutely shows the leg in question was once attached to the human body of Moses Four Bears—and I don't believe any testimony has made that absolutely clear—does that mean the descendants of Moses Four Bears have absolute right to his leg? Leave behind the emotional convolutions, the generalized conceptions of history, and the philosophical meanderings of the Four Bears' legal advisor and what do you have? A museum in the possession of the leg. A museum staff that went to great lengths to acquire and preserve the leg in the state in which Mr. Williams found it. Furthermore, what makes the testimony of the Native witnesses dubious are stories, remembered events outside the facts of ownership. The museum bought the leg, the museum possesses the leg, the museum owns the leg. Another famous philosopher countered the previously mentioned philosopher's statement with "The result is the beginning." In this case the result is the museum has possession of the leg. Thank you, your Honor.

Salazar: After hearing the testimony and following the flow of arguments of counsel on both sides, I must side with the Four Bears family. In my mind, the testimony of Mrs. Four Bears and Mr. Oshawa- nung was convincing. And I saw no motive for them to desire the return of a leg that had no connection to their personal history as tribal people. The testimony of the museum curator and Dr. Williams, on the other hand, provided no real motive for displaying the leg or possessing the leg. The function of the museum will not be dramatically affected by loss of the leg; after all, the museum staff can reproduce a whole person in dress similar to what Mr. Four Bears might have worn. As for the legal issue, while I real- ize that the leg doesn't technically exist as buried remains—it is not a bone—I believe you could make the case that the leg falls under the category of human remains. Flesh has never been precluded in such categories, so clearly I am not making a big legal leap when I say that state and federal repatriation laws on Native American remains are relevant in my decision. I rule in favor of the Four Bears; the mu- seum must turn the leg over to the family in ten days. That should give museum personnel enough time to produce a model leg, if the museum so desires.

(Nugush whispers to his client, Mr. Post.)

Salazar: Are there any final comments before we close the case?

Cage: No. Thank you, your Honor.

Nugush: Your Honor, I have a few comments, and if the court is open, a suggestion.

Salazar: Proceed.

Nugush: While my client and I understand the points of your decision, though we don't agree with them, we believe there is another alternative course to pursue, pertaining to the matter of whether the leg in question belonged to Moses Four Bears or not. My client told me that we can determine, absolutely, if the leg belonged to Mr. Four Bears by exhuming his body to match the leg with the body. Scientific procedure and exhumation would give us the clearest indication of one of the issues central to our being here. This process would benefit not only the court, in rendering an absolutely clear decision, but it might also benefit the Four Bears' family, since they could be absolutely, or at least more, certain that they have the right leg.

Salazar: Mr. Nugush, Mr. Post, thank you for your consideration, not only for the court, but for the Four Bears family, but I believe most of us are sure about the identity of the leg. Exhumation won't be necessary. My decision stands.

AFTER THE REQUIEM

Night fell as the old man slept in the back of the car at the side of Oshawa. The road ran gray in the headlamps of the yellow car, and the voices of the radio came out of a thin mask of lit numbers and lines above a wisp of smoke peeling away from a cigarette in an ashtray. At times Oshawanung's lips moved and his eyelids danced and Oshawa felt the semblance of a gesture in the old man's dream traveling in the night.

At a stoplight, in a town just off the reservation, the old man woke. Oshawa reached into his pocket and took out the painted stone. He measured his words in the dark and spoke to the old man from a face that ran reflective against a window of stars.

"We're almost home, Uncle," the young man said.

Oshawanung reached up over the front seat. "Pass me a smoke, I'm awake now."

In the front seat his son, the driver, reached into his right coat pocket and held the cigarette over his shoulder without moving his eyes from the road, without taking his left hand from the top of the black wheel. The old man struck a match and Oshawa saw the man brightly then, and then he saw the same darkness before the match flame, consummating the return of shadows in the smell of a burning Camel, unchanged but for a few embers glowing more intensely with more intense inhalations of his smoking uncle.

The young man spoke again. "Remember the stone you gave me?"

The shadow nodded, breathing out "Eh heh" in a plume of blue smoke.

"I'm giving it back now. What you said in the courtroom makes me think I should return it now. Pass it on to someone else, another of our relatives, or a Four Bears."

Oshawanung crushed the cigarette out into an ashtray on the door handle beside him. "That stone is yours. You're a descendent of the people the stone was first given to. Your older cousin here," he motioned to the man driving, "he was gone out west when I had the dream about giving the stone away. He knows what the stone means too, but I gave it to you; you who were here on the land."

"But I may have misused the stone," Oshawa said. "I shot at someone once, tried to kill, I put anger in the stone."

OSHAWA'S ATTEMPT TO KILL

Boys were teasing me for a long time. At first I listened and walked away. Then they started setting me
up, they made traps for me and caused me to fall
down in public, they brought me shame. Once after
they made me look bad in front of the whole school,
I chased them. They sang teasing songs as they ran in
different directions. I followed one of them home
then. I kept chasing and chasing him. We ran up that
hill overlooking the mission. Near a house up there I
thought I had him trapped. I took out the stone and
I held it, aiming at the boy with my slingshot. He
moved behind a tree, so I listened, waiting for him
to move. When he didn't, I moved quietly up toward
the tree. All the while I held my slingshot ready to
fire. I saw him on the other side of the tree sneaking
away with his back to me. I took aim, but he looked
back and saw me and then he ducked around the corner of the house. When I got to the other side of the
house, I saw him as the sun glared off of a big window and blinded me, but as it did I heard the boy's
voice coming out of the sunlight, so I shot the stone
in the direction of the voice, toward a tree where I
thought he was standing. The stone struck the tree
and bounced off into the window. That boy Two Birds
ran away laughing and I ran away and left the stone.
When I went back the next day I found a dead bird
at the bottom of the tree. Then a few days later I went
to the door of the house and asked the woman who
lived there if I could have the stone back.

ROSE MESKWAA GEESHIK'S
AFTER-IMAGE DREAMS

I gave the stone back to the boy. His story in some
way reminded me of the way I'd come back to the
reservation. I was looking like you are, looking for
something I was sure I'd left behind when I went to
the city. With the boy gone and the stone in his
hands again, my dreams of the little man faded out,
not all at once, but in increments back to the issues of
my own work. I could remember the inside of every
dream I had of the little man, and the dream was
good enough. I went back to painting, to the images
that I couldn't grasp to release. Initially that meant
a series of faceless abstracts of the colors I'd seen
between myself and the person of stone memory.
Then I was looking out from someone else's eyes to
make landscapes of the mission, landscapes of the
tree outside my window. The tree grew higher in my
painting to a point where I put the little man of my
dreams, rising from his death platform of my dream,
painting the undersides of clouds with the subtle
faces of all the people I'd seen go into the ground
since I'd returned. In winter I painted a Windigo eat-
ing the crosses off the graves. This scared me, especially when Leon came into my room—first as a man,
then as a child. Then I found myself inside his grave
house, drifting through photographs. The grave
house was filled with them, photographs of war,
of warriors, photographs of men hiding in trees. So
there are death portraits I tried to complete, and to
overcome my fear I went to look at the grave houses

one morning. When I got to the burial site I found
that a tree had fallen on top of one of that group of
houses out by Megis Lake. The top of that house was
crushed. It was then that I received word that my
father was sick. I came to take care of him and found
him unconscious. Alive but unconscious. Yes, he
speaks sometimes through his fever, but the words
are scattered, Anishinabe fragments. Arthur, when
you slept he spoke out: "*Anday ishaw ahyen, come back,
Noka, Ojeeg, Maingance, Amikwa, Ahkeewaynzee Kinew,
Abetung, Geezhis, Geeshik Eway Abaht, Quayzaince
Nimkee, Kahbemubbe, Minogeshig, come back . . .*"

ARTHUR BOOZHOO
TWO DOGS STUCK TOGETHER

When Rose came to this part of her story a boy from
the village came up to the house. He spoke quickly
and out of breath from running.

"I'm looking for old man Seed," he said. "We need
him down at our place. Someone said he'll know
what to do."

"He can't go," Rose told him. "The old man is sick,
too sick to go anywhere. Come back in a few days;
maybe he'll be better then."

"We need someone now," the boy went on.
"There's a problem there right now."

"I'll go," I said. "I've been working with the old
man for a while, maybe I can help out."

The boy turned then and ran up Seed's two-track
toward the road. I left Rose and followed quickly
without running, yet keeping the running boy in my
sight. In time I saw him ascend a hill up near
Weaver's, to a field just beyond the village school. He
crested the hill and disappeared. When I reached the
hill, I looked down and saw a group of children in a
circle on the field below, just this side of the school
road, not too far from Squandum's driveway. From
where I stood I could make out two dogs in the center
of the circle. The details grew clearer as I came to the
perimeter of the circle, a mangy long-haired white
mongrel mounted, dancing on two legs, at the rear
end of a brown dog.

As I broke through the circle of children, one of

them, a little girl in a Smurf T-shirt, looked up at me, pleading, "Do something, they're stuck together."

My first thought was to pull them apart, but the futility in this became apparent when I became a part of the dog dance and when one of the older boys said, "We tried that already."

"Maybe we should just leave them alone," I said. "They'll come apart sooner or later."

"We tried that too." Another little girl spoke up this time. "They've been this way for a long time now."

Then I remembered magic, my sideline vocation, my years of training. First I tried mental magic: I attempted to project the image of a piece of meat into the mind of the dancing white dog. For a minute I thought it worked, since I heard the white dog give off a low growl and I thought I saw his mouth water. But the dogs remained stuck together. Then I resorted to displacement, the magic of moving one physical presence to another place with the idea that the whole reality would change as the designated dog moved; at least, that is the way I explained it to the children. Then I told one of the children to get me a blanket. The Weaver boy ran off again and went into one of the white HUD houses nearby. He came back out with a thin blanket with southwestern Indian designs on it.

"Good," I said as I took it from him. Then I walked over, threw the blanket on top of the dogs, and said these words: "Beshig, neesh, nisway, neewin, ho wah." The dogs danced more violently under the blanket. They darted around inside the circle in spo- radic bursts with rodeo leaps, with the passion of lovers lost in passion, but when they bucked the blanket off into the air, they were still locked together. I searched inside for more ideas, for some way of separating the white mongrel and the brown mutt, but I too was stuck.

A pickup stopped on the road nearby then, and one of those young LaVerve boys got out of the truck and walked toward us. I remembered meeting him a year or so earlier, when his father, the minister at the Episcopal church, came to my place to inquire about my religious beliefs and magical practices.

"What the hell's going on here?" LaVerve said.

In his walk and in the difficulty and dramatic intensity with which he spoke I sensed something strange brimming out of his measured behavior. When he came closer I smelled it, sixteen Grain Belts or an unholy number of whiskies.

"The dogs are stuck together." I pointed to the obvious.

"They can't be stuck that much," he said. "I bet I could pull those sons-a-bitches apart myself."

Without going into the history of my efforts or into his inappropriate use of the word "bitches," I watched him try. I watched him dance the same dance I had danced, only he danced with a different personal vigor of drunken actions and breathless curses. After a few futile minutes he turned to me.

"You grab that white bastard and I'll pull on this brown bitch."

I followed his instructions, pulled with all my might while he pulled until his face flushed into rage as the brown dog bit him on the wrist.

"Dammit," he said. "Enough's enough."

Then he walked back toward the blue pickup parked on the road, opened the door on the passenger side, and took a rifle off the gun rack above the seat.

"No," one of the children said from behind me, "don't do it," and she raced up and embraced the dog.

"Get the hell out of the way," LaVerve shouted. Then he ripped the girl away from the dog, took aim, and shot.

"This'll get them apart," he said, firing one more time, as blood boiled up from the places where the bullets struck the white dog.

But the only thing that changed was the dog dance; the white dog whimpered as he remained fast to the brown female, following behind her in a more frantic dance that still failed to separate them. So LaVerve set down his gun and pulled again with his hands, furiously, ignobly bloodying his own hands in wasted effort. Breathless, he gave up, returned to his truck, and turned into a silhouette at dusk, drinking heavily from a sundown bottle, lifted from between his legs, before he drove off.

"You kids go home now," I said. "I'll take care of these dogs for you."

As I said that I looked right at the little girl who had tried to stop the drunken LaVerve. I lifted the dogs and walked back to Seed's place. When I got there it was dark but for a bright moon pouring down onto his front porch. Just as a cricket fossilized against the moonlight jumped from the porch rail, I saw Seed, sitting in a chair there, next to Rose. He made a move to rise, but I stopped him.

"No, stay there." I hauled the dogs over and laid them out on the porch. "They've been stuck like this for a long time," I said, "Those Weaver kids and a few others wanted me to get them apart, but I couldn't. Jimmy LaVerve came along and shot the white one. As you can see, it didn't help."

Seed studied the two dogs. He spoke without looking up at me. "We've got to get this dead one off before he stiffens up." Seed slid out of his chair then and leaned over the dead white dog. He whispered into the dog's ear. I didn't hear the words or the language, but when he settled back into his chair he told me to take the white dog out and bury it. I did as he told me, and I expected the white dog to remain fast to the brown, but when I lifted the dead dog the two dogs separated and the brown dog ran off into the darkness. I went out, picked Seed's shovel from against the woodpile near a shed out back, and started digging. As I dug and as the hole got bigger and deeper, I still couldn't separate in my mind the living dog from the dead dog or the white dog from the brown dog. I couldn't separate those dogs and I couldn't reconcile the failure of my illusions about magic with the physical form I dropped into the hole I'd dug.

Arthur Boozhoo stopped in his story then, rubbed his fingers together as he put a velvet cigarette into his mouth with his left hand and whispered out "megwetch" when Oskinaway's grandfather handed him a lighter. Oskinaway's eyes were sleepy cracks by then as he drifted toward his own magical encounter with a childhood dream. But before he reached the place where dream fluid thought emerged, where waking solid thought dissipated, Boozhoo began again, and the substance of his words drew the boy away from any magical doorway he was about to enter.

This is only part of what Seed asked me to tell you. In four days, if you want Seed to try to see where or who your parents are, you should come to his place at dusk. Bring tobacco, bring a cloth.

SEED'S JOURNEY TO THE CAVE

When they returned to Seed's place, four days later, the old man led the boy and his grandparents out behind the house to the top of a hill. From there the boy saw the village alive in the sundown light. A few cars sputtered away in puffs on the road, running along the river; the voice of old women called children in from the shadows; cranes angled by overhead, barely visible but formed together, distinct in the last tinges of red light in the air.

"Do you have your cloth?"

Oskinaway handed the cloth and the tobacco to Seed. Seed whispered a prayer, tied the tobacco into the cloth, and walked over to a huge tree, where he hung the cloth to a low branch. At a faint nod, Arthur followed the old man and motioned for the rest of the participants to do the same. They circled the tree four times, then Seed lay down on a blanket, where Boozhoo wrapped him up and tied him with rope. He then assisted the old man by putting him into a frame lodge, where the old man stood up, wrapped and tied. Then Boozhoo covered the whole frame with heavy brown canvas. As Boozhoo sang, voices came out of the lodge, turning rapidly in the air, in swift unintelligible words. Suddenly Seed was among them again, unwrapped, bending down at the base of the lodge offering tobacco. The people sat there on the ground then while Seed and Boozhoo smoked.

Then Seed began. "Your mother is alone now in the city. Trains are passing overhead and she sleeps

against a concrete wall now. If you try to find her you
won't get there in time. But someday when you are
older, she will come back to you in a nonhuman form
and teach you about healing and language. As for
your father, I heard stories about him, and though
the stories seem hard to follow, or unrelated, there is
a trail. Part of the trail is in your name, part of the trail
is marked next to the name of your ancestors, with an
X. Look for Abetung, he who inhabits, like the X on
a treaty document. This same X makes us related too.
The man you are looking for is descended from a
more distant Seed.

"But the story goes on: When I was in the lodge
a boy came to me. He took me by the hand, and we
crossed the river. There was a trail there marked by
songs, the remembrances of stones, the bend of certain trees. I followed the boy on this trail for a long
time. I grew tired and I felt myself aging the farther
I traveled on the trail.

" 'Keep moving,' the boy said. 'Don't stop, don't
look back, and don't take anything. We must leave
everything as we found it here. Keep moving, old
man.'

"I did what the boy said, and in time, after a long
time, after the sun fell back behind us into darkness,
we came to a high place on the edge of the river
where the boy went down the side of a cliff while
hanging onto a rope that was tied to an old tree. I
watched as he descended into an opening in the cliff;
then he was gone into the mouth of the cave there.
I stood waiting until I heard his voice.

" 'Come on. Keep moving.'

"For a moment I doubted the boy's purposes. The
rope was thin, and I saw the river washing moon-

light, glimmering thick and heavy far below. I didn't
want to go. I was thinking of other things—of warm
fires and relatives back in the village. I saw the whole
of the village in my mind, from sunrise to sundown.
I was about to turn and run when the boy called
again.
" 'Take the rope and come down,' he said. 'Keep
moving. We can't stay up there where you are. Keep
moving.'
"I took the rope and braced myself against the high
rock face of the river's edge. As I went down I heard
a flute song rising up above the churning voice of the
river, and as I descended further, the song grew
louder and more beautiful. When I made the mouth
of the cave, the last hollow echoes of the flute faded
into the laughter and the muffled voices of a man and
a woman, far below, invisible on the riverbank somewhere. At that moment the boy helped me into the
cave, and when I turned to the inside of the cave I
made out the shadow of another, inside the cave,
beyond the lick and glow of a small fire, across from
where the boy had made a place for himself on the
ground.
" 'Sit down, neegie,' the man said, 'over here
where it is warmer.'
"I did as the man said, and as I approached the fire
and sat down, I saw a bowl of water, a flat grinding
stone, and I saw that he was working something
in his hands. I watched as he worked and waited
for him to speak. The weariness I had forgotten in
my descent down the river cliff returned all at once
as I sat within the warmth of the fire during those
moments. But as I felt myself drifting off, the man
reached out, with his hand, just beyond the outer

edges of the fire, and he placed a small human figure
there, propped up against a few stones of the fire
ring. As he did this, his face came closer to the fire,
and I could see that he was not old. His hair shone
black in the firelight, and his face held taut to his
youth. I also noticed gashes and deep scars on his
forehead as he reached down again to make sure
the figure was propped up securely near the fire.
He spoke then as his face moved back into shadow,
as he sat back upright away from the fire.

" 'Tomorrow's people are here now,' he said.
'Most of them will look back in time and say,
"Remember the old ways; remember the beginning,
the stories and the prophecies." Some will point to
physical remnants in the mnemonic designs of ancestors, and maybe they will trace these designs to the
otter, and further to the bear, who broke through and
made the trail to this land. Others will remember
those who turned to stone and remained far away
where they heard stories from a great stone. Others
will find the stories in language, in the way language
leads back to stones and animals, speaking among
the little people, who first shaped the stones for us
and who inhabit the rock faces and who can become
part of those rock faces in ways most eyes can't dis-
cern. Still others will mourn for what they can't get
back, as if what was given once can never be given
again.

" 'I tell this to you, old man,' he said, gesturing to
the boy beside him, 'because my son is listening and
he takes this as truth. But between us, I can't say that
I have done enough to let him understand the truth.
I live in this cave; each day I descend to the river and

I take mud and clay, and each night I bring this clay
back and work it with stone and water and I mold
human figures around hollow bark frames, out of the
earth. When I'm finished, when the figures I make
have hardened at the edge of this fire, I give each
figure a survival or spiritual name and an engraved
mark that represents their name. Then I take them
to the mouth of the cave and try to drop them into
the river below. Some of these figures do not reach
the water. If I don't concentrate and drop the figure
without thinking, they fall and lodge, immobile, in
the mud or grass below. I've found a few who have
shattered against rock. Sometimes I don't gauge the
wind. Others fall into the river and sink, for who
knows what reason; perhaps a crack formed in the
hardened clay, or maybe the bark interior has some
natural defect that destroys their buoyancy. A good
many of these people go on, though, floating along
the river into tributaries and lakes, into sandbars,
onto islands. And quite often, the people who live
below pick these figures up and take them away.
From there I know some are sold. I know because I
send my son to the villages once in a while to look in
on what people are doing, how they are living. He
told me one man out there has made a life for himself
by trading for the people we make. He pays the
finders and displays the figures all around his place
of business.

" 'But this probably means nothing to you. I feel
you can't imagine why I make these things, why I
work in solitude, deep in the woods, outside the purpose of the general flow of human life. As I said, the
people of tomorrow are here now in what we do and

say. I know because my son here is one of them, and there is a boy you yourself know who has exactly the same face. I know because I was part of his making too. When I was younger a woman gave herself to me for my healing. She warmed me, kept me from freezing in the house of an old man named Geeshis. When the woman gave birth, my grandmother told me to take the first twin away from the village. We had to do it, she said. We had to take the first twin away. We may bring him back when everything is returned to us.'

"The sculptor moved then, from his place by the fire, and walked to the mouth of the cave. He gazed out into the darkness for a few minutes, and I saw his mouth moving as he whispered out into the air.

" 'The sun is coming up,' he said. 'The figure by the fire is ready.' Then he nodded to the boy, 'You take this one, son. You drop this one.'

The boy walked around the fire, picked up the clay man, and waited near his father by the cave opening. I walked up, too, and stood next to the father and son. As the first sign of sun spread out over the land, I saw a cool mist masking the face of the river. Then the boy threw the sculpture out of the cave a ways, where it began its descent. For a few seconds the falling object was a man shining in sunlight, the color of the earth he came from. Then the accumulating speed of his descent turned the man into a vague form, distinct from his surroundings, but distinct only in detachment, in his disconnection from other solid, discernible forms. Then, almost instantly, the figure vanished without a trace in the river mist. There was no human-shaped hole in the cloud over the river. The tiny human was swallowed whole and illogically, as if the clay never was, as if the shape never existed. I left the boy and the man then. I last saw them heading down the riverbank to gather more clay, as I was climbing back up the rock cliff to the path I followed home."

Seed paused for a moment, as Oskinaway's grandmother handed him a cup of tea. He looked into the cup for a moment, then he turned to the boy, Oskinaway: "I believe the man I saw on that journey, the man who spoke to me in that cave, he is your father, and when the time is right you, my boy, will have to find the cave on your own, so you can bring that other, the boy who was born just before you, out of the world of secrets, out of the invisible unknown, back to the village. By then your father will live only for making his little human forms, and he will see them as the family he shouldn't have let go of, and he will let go of the family he should have made. Perhaps the things I've told you here will take care of your dreams, as will some songs you will receive from other dreams." Seed stood up in the darkness and walked away into a shadow and then into the bent luminous figure of a man passing under an infested porch light. The old ones followed, as did Arthur Boozhoo.

The boy stayed behind, staring out into the darkness, moving his eyes into the clear sky above him, glancing once in a while into the woodland night, knowing the animal eyes of others on him, from a hidden beyond. Then just before his grandfather came back for him, and drew him out of his attention to the depths of darkness, the boy heard a song.

The song of Oskinaway

Distant Seed,
out of light,
remember the last voice,
the voice of the people,
the force, and speak
of illumined faces,
a heart hungry for home calls,
through Squandum, beyond Abetung

cranes rise again

WE THE PEOPLE

Oskinaway was tired of working with people. He'd
seen enough. He'd seen elders and children go cold,
shivering on the road to the tribal offices as he and
other tribal employees passed in new blue-and-red
vehicles with the Fineday tribal logo and tribal motto
shining forth in the north country sun, with words
and images that covered the whole native state of
Minnesota in magnitudinous brightness and official
integrity. He'd also seen money changing hands—
red to white to red to white—in an unchecked flow
between council officials, all their relations, government agents, bingo lawyers, and a thousand consorts
of these types in the form of consultants.

"These are the days of special interest," one of
the council members, Sean Strawberry, once said as
Oskinaway filled the tank of a tribal vehicle at Strawberry's twenty-four-hour gas, beer, wine, and video
station, The Restless Native. "Yes, and in order to
maintain our sovereign status as an independent
nation, we must ascertain the interests that will pro-
liferate our specialness." Oskinaway signed the gas
voucher and left amazed, to wonder in the beauty of
the world along the reservation road, in the sunflash
of crow wing, in the vacillation of yellow-headed
blackbird from bullrush to jerky flight under a sky of
thick white clouds, rubbing against the highest green
hills, beyond even the aspirations of the greatest of
tamaracks—to wonder if the place he'd just left and

the place he was going were one and the same as the road he was traveling on.

After a particularly frustrating morning in the dead of winter when Oskinaway had to explain a form letter to a traditional elder face to face, to clarify why, in accordance with program guidelines that were vague even to him, the elder and her grandchildren were being denied home heating assistance, wonder ceased for him. It was gone especially, a few days later, when Oskinaway looked out the window of the Health and Human Services building after work hours, in near darkness, and saw councilman John Smith LaRock back his Dakota up to the loading dock and fill the back end with commodities and at least a half cord of wood, intended for tribal members deemed economically eligible by government guidelines for home heating assistance. Oskinaway's fatigue overcame him in a realization of his own fatuous endeavors, feeding one after another on vague ideals and unfulfillable self-promises, and he decided at that moment to leave, to work toward a life that he'd turned over in his mind for at least as long as he saw the road in his memory leading him to the doorway light of the Methodist hall, where so many old people sang around the body of a youth found frozen in a ditch, dead according to various rumors and theories by overdose, suicide, accident, lack of self-esteem, the urgency of youth, the urgings of peers, lack of communication, lack of direction, lack of spirit. And even as the old ones sang for the spirit, at that time, Oskinaway first considered moving on, to continue his education, to work with animals instead of people.

In the fall of the fiftieth year of the seventh fire,

with a tribally backed financial aid package, he
enrolled in veterinary college at Michigan State
University.

He did well. The course work moved him to
continue. He saw clear through the theory to days
beyond even internship when practical applications
would remedy the greatest and smallest afflictions of
animals in his hands. Some would die, he knew, but
those he saved would move on to stir the world a bit
more with the unique habits of one more being living
a natural existence. As he studied veterinary texts,
inside himself he saw a white fox bounding on a doc-
tored leg on a hillside; he saw blue herons striding
back to rivers after being untangled from the lines of
careless fishermen; he saw black horses giving birth,
a trembling colt standing in a pasture at dawn; he
saw a yellow dog returning to its people, whole and
alive, bounding into the arms of a child.

In two springs, with such dream sketches drawing
him on, he'd gone far enough in school to petition for
graduation. As he sat before an old Smith Corona,
wine on one side, bologna and cheese on the other,
filling in the blanks, typing the last letters of his
name, the trailer lost power. Lightning and thunder
echoed forth from outside the trailer to shake the thin
walls and all the material, philosophical, and metaphysical hangings within. Oskinaway gave up typing
in the dark, walked the narrow hallway to the back
bedroom of the trailer, and sat down on the bed to
take off his burnt-apple cowboy boots. As he slipped
the left boot off he saw a thin dot of blue light
descend from the corner of the room near the ceiling.
Gradually, the blue light expanded and brightened,
enlivening the room in shape and form to a point

where Oskinaway saw a woman in a blue dress dancing before him. More clearly, he saw hundreds of cowrie shells covering the woman's dress. As she danced, the shells swished rhythmically, silencing the room to every other sound, until Oskinaway heard voices behind the shells, singing forth with faint reverberating drums that drew tears from his eyes and moved him to get up and dance with the woman before she disappeared in predawn dreams.

Morning sun ran through a hole in swift clouds, filtering through the bent and broken blinds of the window in the room where Oskinaway slept. When the light touched his eyelids he came out of sleep and jumped up from the floor, still dressed, with one boot still on his right foot. He looked at the clock, washed, changed clothes, grabbed his backpack, and hurried out the door to his first class that morning. As he walked he noticed how the power of storm had broken trees and strewn branches across campus roadways and paths. He saw dead, wet leaves, soaked newspaper blown from human hands, and drenched announcements ripped from bulletin boards, matted against concrete and asphalt. When he came to the center of campus, near the bell tower, he marked time mentally at the big painted stone.

In the years he'd been at Michigan State he'd taken note of the stone, the changes it went through. At least twice a year the whole stone changed color. Once it was painted red, then it was gold, and there were always names, numbers, and Greek letters there. Sometimes inventive lovers left messages that miraculously lasted through new coats of paint. Sometimes, after studying for hours at the library, Oskinaway would take a break and walk back to the stone and read everything on it, word by word, letter by letter. As he did he wondered, Who painted the stone? Who changed it from one color to another? Was this a stone for fraternities and lovers only? He wondered because he knew that almost everyone on campus passed by the stone, but he never saw anyone near the stone, much less painting the stone. Oskinaway had no idea how or when the stone was painted. Then, as he came even with the stone on the path, as he took note that it was yellow this time, that someone had repainted it recently, he saw something resting on top of the stone. He walked off the path to the stone and saw a bird. The bird was breathing, but not moving. When he was close enough, he reached out to touch the bird, but when his hand made contact with the slick black-feathered body, the bird's beak shot out with a quick, violent strike to the back of Oskinaway's other hand, where it ripped off a piece of flesh and left Oskinaway bleeding in surprise. Oskinaway backed off quickly and sat under a nearby tree. A few minutes later, after internal voices recalled lessons learned in the university animal psychology classes and teachings of his grandparents and tribal elders about approaching and speaking to animals, Oskinaway returned to the bird on the stone.

"Boozhoo . . . Ahneen andayk
makaday beneshay
makaday beneshay andayk makaday
     beneshay
beneshay makaday andayk

Indishnikawz Oskinaway neegie
Beshig, neezh, nissway, neegie

neewin, nahnnahn, neegie

How far is it to Mexico, friend?
Are you sleeping on the wing?"

He spoke softly, slowly, so the words worked
almost to singing in his mind and so the words
stretched language to the mind of the bird and turned
the bird to trust Oskinaway. Then Oskinaway lifted
the bird into his hands and scanned the bird's body
from top to bottom; in the continuance of his song-
whisperings, he saw that the bird had a bad wing.
Then Oskinaway remembered who he was and
where he was, so at once he decided to take the bird
with him, to find a way to heal the bird. He took the
red bandana off his head, gently wrapped it around
the bird, stuck the bird in his backpack, and continued on to his eight o'clock class at the veterinary college. The bird sang briefly as they passed beneath
phoebes nesting under the eaves of the university's
natural history museum.

When he arrived at the classroom, he went to the
back of the class, opened a window, and sat in the
last row near the open window. This was his plan for
shifting attention should the bird decide to sing during lecture: he would look out the window as if the
sounds of the bird were outside the room instead
of inside. As it turned out, the bird cried just once,
when three crows whirled down onto the branch of
a silver maple that extended into the framed view
of the classroom window. Oskinaway acted out his
plan, but apparently no one else seemed to notice—
although the professor did pause, in both his lecture
and the examination of the shine on his shoes, to look

up and catch a glimpse of the traffic on a nearby road, as the bird's voice sawed through an opening in the backpack.

As for the lecture, time stood still in a flood of abstractions, in a spiritless dissertation on animal physiology. Oskinaway looked and heard, like so many other students in such a situation, but he took in nothing. His mind wandered to dinner options, to possible solutions for healing the bird, to reservation homes, to the northern river where his grandfather, old man Squandum, fished with him and gave him stories and songs. The academic vacancies didn't matter in the retrograde musings where Oskinaway grew to learn from the old people. He saw how the grandparents he grew up with took in people even older than themselves. How they'd hand him plates of boiled potatoes, corn, wild rice, chokecherries, and white bread and send him out into a frigid darkness, to walk a narrow path in hard snow to the shacks where the ones who were even older than his grandparents lived. Once, when he stooped down to enter, he would see through another doorway the old man, blue sparks of light emitting from his eyes, sitting on the edge of an iron bed in dim light, and he would shout across the room until the old man rose and came to sit at the table where the food waited. For a long time he never knew the man's name or why he was there; he just knew he was his grandmother's relative. Sometimes he'd try to talk to the old man as he rekindled the stove, or as he waited for him to finish his food, but the conversations ran cryptic between Ojibway and English and memories flashing forth from the old man's mouth as quickly as images through the human mind to a slower tongue. Yet there were glimpses of understanding: once the old man spoke as he looked deeply into thick snow falling in the shadows of pines outside the window.

"I can see those Sioux moving over there across the lake."

Another time, he told the boy about thunders and putting tobacco down, but again, what Oskinaway grasped among the many words seemed like a breath of mist in a whole fog. And when he returned to his grandmother with the old man's empty plate, he never thought to ask her about what the old man said, or why she was feeding him. But somehow he'd learned from her, and all the old ones—through gesture and act, those unspokens that travel within and without human interaction—that helping has meaning, as names have meaning. So years later when the old man died he read the name on the headstone OSKINAWAY and he thought to ask. The old woman told him, "This is who you are named for." And as memory returned him to his own name and what he'd learned, the classroom of students trudged out to the last forgotten words of the professor's lecture.

When everyone else was gone Oskinaway approached the professor. "Do you have a minute?"

Oskinaway took off his backpack, carefully extracted the bird, unwrapped it and set it down on the table. "Can it be healed?" he asked.

The professor looked up from the hands on silver hinges of his black briefcase, then looked at the bird. He spoke as his eyes worked along the length of the bird's body, back and forth a few times: "Maybe you haven't been listening. You've gotta start thinking domestic or farm. We've made no mention of wild

animals in this class or any other class in this program. This bird is a wild bird."

With that the professor lifted his briefcase and
walked out, leaving Oskinaway momentarily dis-
couraged and wholly confused.

Once again Oskinaway wrapped the bird and put
it in his backpack. On the way home he noted the
ascension of a few crows from a smashed raccoon
in the alley behind the trailer park. He watched the
movement of their wings, the bend and angle of
those wings as they stroked air and stopped to glide,
then to land on the red tile roof of a Mexican restaurant. He studied the crows as they cawed out and
flew off again, and he envisioned the same movements on the bird he carried with him. In those
moments the discouragement of a few words by
his professor turned into a determined drive to
see the bird healed.

The first acts of determination found form in a
room in the trailer, in a cage for the bird. After dark
Oskinaway stole a few metal milk crates from the
back wall of a nearby Kroger's. Then he found some
chicken wire a neighbor had been using to protect
a small plot of tomatoes. With these, a few other
materials, and a twelve-pack of Stroh's in hand, he
approached another neighbor, a laid-off welder, who
constantly bragged of his abilities with an acetylene
torch. By midnight the two of them had created an
expandable, portable cage, complete with a fold-
down door. Oskinaway set this cage up on a table
next to a window that looked out onto a few large
pines and beyond that to a local bar with the E and A
burnt out of its neon GRAIN BELT sign. For the next

few weeks Oskinaway gathered posters and nature
magazine photographs of eagles, vultures, hawks,
crows, of healthy birds in flight, and hung them
up on the walls all around the room where the
bird lived.

Then he began serious study at the university
library. Between classes, after classes, early in the
morning, late at night, he'd study cases, reports,
journals, sketches, photographs, stories, any information he could find on wing injuries and healing
wild birds. Some sources connected him to further
correspondence and firsthand conversations with
veterinarians and volunteers at bird sanctuaries and
wildlife rescue operations throughout the country.
Once he talked by phone to an old fisherman from
Sarasota, Florida, who had tired of seeing pelicans
dying in struggles brought on by confrontations with
fishing lines and hooks. This human concern eventually inspired the fisherman to create a seven-acre
sanctuary for wounded pelicans just off the Sarasota
Bay, complete with spacious cages for the healing
birds that could move but weren't ready to return to
the wild. The sanctuary also included a bird hospital
for recently wounded birds that had just come in to
the sanctuary and needed immediate attention or
more constant care. Oskinaway's conversations with
this man covered subjects ranging from feeding to
healing time, to wing repair, to technological material, and to surgical innovations in the performance of
such repair, as well as the most beneficial time, place,
and atmosphere for conducting such performance,
and names and numbers for reaching and interviewing experts who had conducted operations on
wounded birds. Oskinaway also visited wildlife res-

cue operations, where he spoke with veterinarians and volunteers about all aspects of the proper healing of birds with damaged wings.

After final exams in the spring, Oskinaway received a pink message from the veterinary college. The words read:

Dear Mr. Oskinaway:
Your grades have fallen below the minimum standards required for enrollment in the Michigan State University Veterinary College.

He didn't have to read further. He knew the gist and the thrust of the words as they diminished into the echo of vacant school hallways with the interpretive volume and substance of his own personal understanding of the importance of the source of echoes. He had spent too much time on one bird. He had wasted too many nights and conversations on a single-minded project that meant nothing to completion of an established intellectual course.

When he returned to the reservation he found the old place, his grandparents' home, just as it had been when he had lived there alone after they died. He rolled up the overgrown two-track driveway in a blue Nova with a small U-Haul trailer jiggling from the back bumper. He brought the bird in first and set up the cage in the room where his grandmother had slept. He moved through every room with new thoughts about old subjects. In the kitchen he sat down at the rickety wooden table where the old man used to sit. He felt words move through him once again with the substance of the old man's smoking image, coursing through a haze of steaming deer meat, deep bowls of yellow corn, mahnomin brown and wet, glistening as if the wet heat rising from the boiled potatoes had settled onto the rice. Full and nourished in memory, after dinner, he saw blue tobacco smoke in the air, twisting through door frames to the drying medicine hanging on the walls in proximate rooms and to gestures of the old woman's hands on the cabinet door as she reached up to gather evaporated milk and sugar for the tea she had set before them. Then he stood from that place and opened the cabinet himself to see if he could feel the memory in the enamel knobs, to examine the inside of the cabinet, where even in the blindness of later years the old woman still knew where to find the cups and plates and the cans of evaporated milk with the boxes of government-issue foods and the bags of rice. Inside he found nothing. Thick dust covered tacked-down clear plastic on newspapered shelves, and the wood was warped, splintering and drawing away from itself on the cabinet's inner panels. Oskinaway looked and reached further into the empty space. Then he saw words and pulled back the plastic on the shelving. There were layers upon layers of brittle yellow newspaper, each layer older than the layer before. He read parts of each layer until he reached the paper covering the wood. He read the words: they were parts of *The Progress,* a turn-of-the-century reservation newspaper. He recognized a family name there. He turned dates over in his head. He held up fragments.

> Minogeshig . . . Old traditions must die . . .
> Survival as a people . . . on educating . . .
> ourselves . . . Indian . . . in accordance . . .

white man . . . lumber . . . Nelson Act . . .
the mission . . . births . . . Wabonoquat . . .

He found more fragments of other newspapers:

the *Minneapolis Journal* . . . 1907 . . . one cent
. . . mad dog is shot in university classroom
. . . bordering on the reservation . . . trusts
surrender as Garfield acts . . . Working the
red man . . . on oil king's trail . . . already
more than 250 allotments have been mort-
gaged for a song—the Indian agent power-
less . . . land speculators responsible for
orgies . . . Halts thaw probe; plea of insanity
. . . little chance for redemption . . . mixed
bloods mortgage land . . . this number
applies to . . . stamps out revolt . . .

He pieced the brittle fragments together into whole
paragraphs on the table. Then he worked the larger
pieces into two-page spreads. When he had pieced
together every part of every page he had, he saw that
the old people had kept allotment records under the
dishes on the shelves. He pored through the names
on the thin paper, and he noticed a few underlined
with red marker. Among the names of his grandparents and great-grandparents he saw the name
Abetung, the name of his father, underlined like all
the rest. He got up from the table and placed the
allotments in the ancient newspapers on top the
dresser in the living room. Then he unloaded his
belongings, which included textbooks and volumes
of animal diagrams. These he set on top of the news

articles to hold them down until he could come up with the materials to put the old papers together and preserve them.

Then he went to a drawer where, a few years before the last time he'd left, he'd stashed a pouch of Velvet tobacco as an offering to protect and preserve the old place, and he sat to smoke, for the first time in years. He sat near the wood stove in the largest room and took in the faces of the dead still on the walls, the missing marines, the ballplayers, the trophies, the cat clock, the broken radio, the Jesuses on crosses and in pictures, the red-willow baskets, the birchbark winnowing basket, the old man's buffalo plaid hat, the blue chair, the mirror where he saw himself for the first time, the old woman's shawl, her sewing tin, and he felt the weariness of his journey as his eyes moved into the stars outside a window across the room. He imagined being born here as he was once, long ago beyond the reaches of his conscious calling. He drew his eyes back from the sky and concentrated on the voices outside. In the dwindling space of closing eyelids, nighthawks rang out, in their silent spaces frogs banded together, syncopating croaks, glazing starlit in slithering and short jumps from swamps and creekbank; incessant crickets filled the spaces between these voices, invisible as hands turning the keys and wheels of distant engines on the roads in and out of the village. He left himself alone then, put out his smoke against the black shadow of the stove, and went to sleep watching his grandmother's blue dress, in thin evening breezes breathing through the open windows, swaying back and forth from the ceiling above.

The next morning Oskinaway met with the tribal

social service director to explain his situation and ask
for temporary emergency assistance. After he filled
out the required forms, Rose Meskwaa Geeshik gave
him vouchers for food and lodging. She also mentioned an opening in the tribal youth services program and told him to check down at personnel for
more information. On his way down, Oskinaway
saw Goldie Kinew leading her blind grandfather
into the clinic. He caught her just outside the
doorway.

"Goldie, how is it?"

"The old man's going fast," she said. "He dreams
full-time now. You know, the conversations, old stories, old songs, different places, names of the dead,
invisible dogs, things like that."

Oskinaway stepped aside to allow the tribal
nurse to pass between them, through the doorway.
"Remember everything, there's a lot there. What is
he, ninety-five now?"

Goldie looked at him strangely, as his words
floated out at her incomprehensible from behind his
eyes. "I don't know—a hundred and twenty-five,
according to tribal records, but I'm not sure even he
knows. Look," she said. "I've gotta go, he has an
appointment and bingo starts at noon. I'm selling
pull tabs at the door. Call me later." With that she
tightened her grip on old Kinew and turned and
led him to a row of seats along the wall of the
reception room. Oskinaway thought about their
reservation romance as he watched Goldie gently
guide old man Kinew to his seat under a velvet
painting of an eagle dragging a fish from water
into air.

Then he found his way to the personnel office.

Again after filling out a few forms, the assistant personnel director, Ruth Rock, told him he was in luck;
they were interviewing for the position he was applying for the next day.

After a brief interview, the tribal hiring board gave
Oskinaway the job with the stipulation that he sign
a four-year contract, since he had after all left his
previous positions with the tribe rather abruptly.
Oskinaway signed the contract and began work
immediately—that afternoon.

Initially his work with youth went well. Under his
directorship the tribe implemented after-school recre-
ation programs, arts and crafts workshops, a summer
language program, traditional-values retreats, a
youth/elder oral history home hospice project, dramatic productions in which the youth scripted and
acted out traditional tales, a dancing club.

Planning and developing those activities took
up most of Oskinaway's days. At night Oskinaway
returned home to the bird and continued the cause
of studying to determine how to heal and care for
the bird. He fed the bird as his studies told him. He
picked up road kill and he served appropriate nuts
and grains. He also went beyond convention and
gave the bird wild rice, bologna-and-cheese sand-
wiches, macaroni and cheese, hotdish, rabbit, strawberry pie. Eventually he concluded that the bird
would be healed, but he knew that it would take
time. One expert, who had come to the reservation
from a renowned University of Minnesota program
for repairing wings of injured wild birds and reintro-
ducing them into the wild, assured Oskinaway that it
would take months, perhaps even longer, for the bird

to heal. And even then he said there was no guarantee that the bird would survive in the wild.

"You must go beyond feeding," he told Oskinaway. "Continue to push the bird to getting stronger." With that the expert left sketches of diagrams for exercises that, as he put it, "would maximize the potential for the bird to heal and return to the world it once knew." Oskinaway followed the diagrams and worked the bird through a daily exercise regimen with powwow tapes as background music. Then while reading through a subscription of one of his many bird magazines Oskinaway was struck by a half-page ad.

As he read on, he discovered that a Professor Horace Benbow from a school in California taught birds of various species to talk, including thirteen blackbirds, seven grackles, twenty or so ravens, a bluebird, and so on. Oskinaway figured that since it would take at least a few months for the bird to heal, he would try the program. Rather than let the bird stagnate in mind while the body healed, Oskinaway, as a human of certain indefinable beliefs, conceived of a program for the whole bird. That part of the bird which missed the day-to-day struggle with survival needed work too. Oskinaway sent away for the Benbow language program the next day.

Professor Benbow's talking-bird program relied on music, repetition, and imitation. According to such a system the bird would be subjected to recordings of phrases—set against a musical accompaniment that was scientifically specified in tempo and type— which the bird would then imitate. As the bird mastered each word or phrase, additional phrases and concepts would be added on. Through such a method Benbow had taught over 160 birds how to recite the Preamble to the Constitution of the United States. Benbow further claimed, not only that his method taught birds to talk, but also that if a person worked with one bird long enough, the Preamble to the Constitution would provide such important and varied training that the bird would be able learn more elaborate phrases and more extensive uses of words, as well as understand and think about the words and phrases it learned.

In a few days Oskinaway's communication package arrived. The Benbow program consisted of:
• One musically backed word-by-word, phrase-by-phrase recording of the Preamble to the Constitution of the United States
• A list of instructions, including organized lesson plans, and a lesson-by-lesson timeline for using the program
• A printed copy of the Preamble, so the bird and its caretaker could practice more advanced lessons together
• A stack of communication application and progress charts

- A list of the most common problems Benbow encountered in applying the program, with corrective measures for dealing with those problems
- A list of Benbow's publications as follows:
  1. *Music and Repetition: A New Concrete Phraseology for Instructing Abstract Wingeds*
  2. *The Language of Birds, the Language of Humans: A Comparative Study of Sound, Song, and Transmission of Messages between Species*
  3. *Language and the Phoenix*
  4. *Perception as a Common Barrier in Animal Communication*
  5. *A Higher Perch: A Defense of the Talking, Thinking Bird*
  6. *Words and Departure from the Nest: The Security in Language*
  7. *Messengers to the Kingdom of Intellect: The Benbow Method for Teaching a Bird to Talk*
- A computerized list of the names and addresses of all the people who had successfully implemented the Benbow method.
- A letter from Benbow himself.

Dear Mr. Oskinaway,

Congratulations! You are a pioneer in animal and human relations. Because of people like you and hundreds of others who have instructed birds in the Benbow method, future human societies will be open to realms of communication unknown to people of our times. We are in fact setting the stage for the birth of an understanding so great and glorious that human knowledge cannot now aspire to the heights our offspring may achieve. Can you imagine speaking to one with the vision of an owl? Can you foresee an interchange of ideas between the architect and the plover? These are just a few of the possibilities a future of communication with the kingdom of wingeds will bring to the human universe. As for now,

work hard and steadily with your bird. If you follow the outline of my program you will see and hear results within a
week. Should the program fail in any way, return your progress charts to me at my laboratories, and I will personally take
time to help you with the implementation of the program.
The best,
Horace Benbow

With the inspiration and excitement of the Benbow
letter still resonating in the evening void of his personal conviction, Oskinaway began immediately. He
took the communication program and all its periph-
erals to his grandmother's room, removed all the
relics of the past from the top of his grandmother's
dresser, and set up the tape recorder, well within
the program-specified distance from the bird.
He set the progress charts and sharpened pencils
next to the recorder, then he nailed the copy of the
Preamble to the Constitution on the wall next to the
window above and behind the dresser.

The tape began with a European largo of harps and
stringed instruments unknown to Oskinaway. Then
a voice flowed forth softly as from a distant harmo-
nium to more voluminous measures of human
speech.

We the People of the United States of America, in
order to form a more perfect union . . .

Oskinaway listened, entranced, understanding
words he knew by sight differently in this first time of
hearing them completely.

Then the voice sighed away momentarily, rose up
on a new wave of music, and began again, more
forcefully.

We (music 1, 2, 3, 4) *We* (music 1, 2, 3, 4)
We (music 1, 2, 3, 4) *We* (music 1, 2, 3, 4)

Oskinaway stripped, glanced at the shining bird
in the moonlight cage, drew the star quilt over
himself, and fell away to sleep with the next
We (music 1, 2, 3, 4).

*"I kill giants. Find me a giant, I'll kill it." The blond
woman screams out with laughter. Next to her a man comes
out of the earth smeared with blood and black wet earth, military medals glistening in thin mist inside a hole of blood in
his breast. The woman draws on a cigarette, floats into a
face behind a missile launcher. An explosion, the man rises
off the ground sucked into thick smoke. The smoke ascends,
expands, rips trees away in its rising. The woman points to
the smoke. "A giant for you, kill it." The giant puts its
enormous smoke head through the ice blue smoke, spits fire
with giant words too loud to understand, deafening giant
burning words.*

*There is a grave house, see through to the inside. All
those photographs. A young man lived there. He is gone
now. He wandered from tree to tree a stoned scout. He was
shot from a tree. They put his uniform on a monkey. They
took photographs. The grave house is full of photographs.
There is his face at the mission school. There he plays
baseball. There he sits with Uncle Anung in the park in
Minneapolis. There he is after Golden Gloves. There he is
graduating. There he is at the June 16 powwow. There he is
with the white girl from Detroit, sitting on her car. There
he is pointing to the rainbow. There he is again and again.
We put food out at the grave house. Even after they lost
the body we put food out for the photographs.*

Within two weeks the bird spoke for the first time. Oskinaway heard the voice as he opened the door of the old people's house one afternoon after work. He rushed into grandmother's room and saw the bird standing in the cage, a backlit silhouette mouthing another inhuman "we" as he entered. Oskinaway approached the cage and spoke to the bird.

"Good," he said. "You said *we*. Now you, we, are ready for more."

With that he began the second side of the tape for the bird. The tempo was the same, but the instruments changed. Oskinaway thought he heard flutes and faint reeds behind the harps. As for the spoken words, "the" accompanied "we."

We the (music 1, 2, 3, 4) *We the* (music 1, 2, 3, 4)
We the (music 1, 2, 3, 4) *We the* (music 1, 2, 3, 4)

At every "we" the bird joined in, voice on top of voice. Oskinaway drew away to sleep, drugged by the repetition.

The river flows red into dawn. Find the missing face, not your face on water as you reach into water to cleanse your face. The face grabs your hand. You're stuck there struggling with all your might with a face pulling you toward the river. You call for help. You hear laughter, a little boy watches you from across the river, a laughing shadow beneath willow. Help me, you say, help me. The little boy has your face. The little boy runs away in fading laughter as the river face finally lets go.

"Kiss me," she says. "It's dark, no one will see." Everyone sees, the blind old man sees, the eye of the theater pro-

jector sees you kiss her through the eyes of the people on the screen. But you can't see. Is it Goldie? Yes, Goldie. No, there is another name carved into wood. But you can't see the name above your name.

By the end of the month the bird had advanced to the first side of the second tape. The bird would say, "We the people." When Oskinaway woke up in the morning, the bird would say, "We the people." When Oskinaway came into the room after work in the evening, the bird would say, "We the people," at almost any time as long as Oskinaway was in the room. So Oskinaway turned the second tape to its second side and a new lesson. While the background music remained essentially the same, but for the addition of widely spaced drum parts, the speaking lesson was much more advanced, with the addition of a phrase instead of just one word.

We the people of the United States (music 1, 2, 3, 4)
We the people of the United States (music 1, 2, 3, 4)

Then somehow the system failed. After two more months the bird still said, "We the people," and "We the people" only. Moreover, Oskinaway realized that the bird spoke those words only at certain times, out of context, instead of every time he was in the bird's presence. It still said, "We the people," when Oskinaway woke up in the morning. "We the people" still rang forth from its beak when he came home in the evening. But the bird also used the phrase whenever Oshkinaway opened the refrigerator or began preparing food. The phrase seemed to have context, but Oskinaway wasn't sure what the context revealed about the bird's understanding of the phrase.

Oskinaway continued faithfully with the fourth lesson for another month. As always, he fell asleep less than minutes into the lesson. But one Friday night he decided to stay awake and sound out the complete lesson with the bird—as stipulated by the troubleshooting steps outlined in Benbow's communication program kit. Halfway through the tape the music stopped. The words had no background. Oskinaway was angry and relieved at the same time. The bird wasn't the problem; Benbow had sent a defective tape.

At work the following morning, Oskinaway ran off the progress reports and drafted a letter to Benbow.

Dear Professor Benbow,
My bird has done well with your program. However, the second side of the second tape is defective. There is no musical background to go with the spoken word. I've enclosed the tape, and I expect that you will either correct the problem or send a new tape. I've also sent copies of the progress reports to show you my committment to your program. Thanks.
Sincerely,
Oskinaway

As Oskinaway signed his name, chairman Two Birds came into the office. He closed the door behind him, lit up a Bull Durham cigarette, and sat in the chair at the desk of the youth program secretary, who had called in sick.

"Boozhoo," he said. "Important meeting one week from today, eight P.M. in the Original Man School gym. I'm giving everyone advance notice, so I expect everyone will be there. Dignitaries from Washington are coming to commemorate the quincentenary of Columbus's arrival in North America. They want this rez to be part of a nationwide celebration. I'd like you to give the welcoming speech."

Oskinaway went blank, inside and out. "Why me? You're the boss. I haven't given a speech since the last tribal election, and you know what happened then."

Speaking through thick smoke, the Bull Durham bouncing in rhythm to every word, Two Birds flew in a different direction, away from even the weakness of the argument. "You've got the biggest education of all the people around here, so be smart, use words those kind of people will hear but not understand because they're coming from someone they don't perceive as an articulate source. You know. Big words, small words, catchwords, let-go words, double-edged words, flat words, skinny words, television words, traditional words, bureaucratic words, radical words in ordinary contexts. Use as many kinds of words as there are Indians on this reservation. Make us proud to hear you without letting us get mad about what you're talking about. Then, after we send those chimooks on their way we have an important tribal matter to discuss. We want everyone there. We're even canceling bingo."

Oskinaway slipped the letter to Benbow into an envelope and set it on the desk calendar in front of him. "Can you clue me in?"

"About what? I told you what to say in the Columbus speech; just don't bring tribal politics into it."

"No, I mean the tribal matter. What is it?"

Two Birds moved his chair back to leave, tapping ashes onto the floor. "Can't say now. We're checking things out, but either way there'll be a meeting." He motioned to the envelope with his head as he pushed out his upper lip. "That's not another resignation is it?"

Before Oskinaway could draw out his wit, Two Birds was out the door, footsteps in the hallway to tribal education. Oskinaway marked his calendar.

Four days later he received a response from Benbow. He opened and read it as he chewed his dinner—macaroni and cheese with a bologna sandwich.

Dear Mr. Oskinaway,

It grieves me to write you that my husband is dead. He died one month ago in a small plane crash in the mountains of Colorado. They have yet to find the body. Moreover, there is no one to continue his work, so I can't help with the defective tape. Try contacting one of the persons listed on the computer printout that came with your program kit. Good luck.

Sincerely,
Willow Benbow

Oskinaway suspended his chewing with his suprise. He thought of Benbow and the voice on the tape. He thought of the man's dream and the pioneer optimism of the first letter he received from Benbow. He left dinner and went to the bird's room. As usual the bird called out, "We the people," when Oskinaway entered the room. Then Oskinaway sifted through the communication packet piece by piece. When he came back to the tapes he picked out the third tape, put it in the machine, sat on the iron bed,

and lit a cigarette. He waited for the music as he followed the shapes of his exhalations. A thin hiss
issued from the machine; no music and no words. He
tried another tape. Again and again he tried, only to
find that every tape in the thirty-two-step program
was blank. He lifted the computer list from the box of
program contents. He called the first number. There
was an automated voice, "This number is no longer
in service. If you . . ." Oskinaway hung up.

Then to shift his attention, he thought of his
Columbus speech. He went to his bed, lit another
self-rolled Velvet cigarette, and began writing. No
words worked well enough in his mind until at some
timeless point he turned to the bird and gazed at the
figure for the first time in a long time. He marveled at
the light the bird held around its body in the sheen of
black feathers, the circumspect drama of its eyes, a
circular band of yellow circles wrapped around light-
specked black centers as it shifted its head from point
to point with a strange animal caution. He wondered
about the strength of the claws, the meaning of the
thin legs. And at once he saw the whole bird as a
source of strength, as a strong healing animal. And
at that point the physical animal turned to human
vision, turning time backward and forward at the
same time as Oskinaway saw himself seeing the
powerful ascension and limitless flight of the bird, of
the past joining with the first tentative spread of wing
by this bird as it rose complete from it own recovery,
to a future strength where its now limited vision
could then encompass expansive landscapes and
myriad movements from heights granted by the
returned power of one wing. Then Oskinaway spoke
his thoughts aloud and wrote them one by one.

One week later, he read his thoughts one by one and spoke them aloud, measuring articulations into the dull house of anticipation in the Original Man gym.

This reservation began as an agreement,
one to another.
For one nation received the right to claim
    lands previously occupied by the other.
The other received 800,000 acres, clearly
    delineated
and set out in the language of
one nation.
The acreage included rivers and numerous
    lakes,
a wealth of flora and fauna, immeasurable
    stands of timber, prairie to the west.
The names beneath the agreement attest
to the promise of the land,
but now the acreage,
the spread of land has changed hands again.
Much of the woodland has been converted
    to board feet,
the rivers are the subject of the magazines
of wild weekends,
the rice on the lakes has been sucked up
in natural resource airboats
and sold in gourmet sections
of distant supermarkets.
As for the prairie,
that too has been fed
by poison, the pesticides
of competition

flow into every creek there, every day.
As for the promise, there are no words.

But to the people of the reservation,
We the organs as nation
are not wholes of survival.
What the lost man sees when he finds land
is not what the land is,
but where he has been
and the direction he thinks he has traveled.

It is no small iron in the industrial fire
still left burning,
that the scientific/European world
    Columbus left,
and the mythical scientific truth he
    destroyed
with his misguided mission,
that the world was flat,
should coincide with floating into a
    hemisphere
in which a great many inhabitants
built the homes, political systems, spiritual
    structures
and values around the round,
the concept of the circle,
the representative concept of the spheres
and cylinders which they saw
with their own vision
from this verdant and holy land.

No noxious fumes informed their words
then as they do now as I speak.
No white birds died black in leaks

from energy ships.
No wastes drove the river's purpose away.
No radiation flared onto the skins
of animals or singed human skin
from human bone in layers
that still melt in celluloid visions
of cultural redemption.
There were no two-headed turtles,
no three-eyed fish,
no man was a mountain of civic pride,
carved into stone.

But still the world is round.
No matter which direction you go.
Five hundred years, like the world traveler,
    will come back around.
Fires will flash, flame, and flicker away
Rivers will swell.
Mountains will take on their own form,
And the turtle will have only one head
but even that won't last,
no, even that won't last as long as the slow
    beating heart.

When Oskinaway came to the heart, he rested in
the silence to survey the faces. The Original Man gym
was packed with families from every village on the
reservation. He looked at the elders, trying to imagine the thoughts behind the eyes; as he looked at the
women attempting to fathom the expressions, the
poses, the gestures, as he looked at the men, he saw
the patterns of appearances diminish in waves of
mixed details from person to person throughout the
huge hollow room. As he looked at the senators in

their seats of honor at a long table, he spoke softly
to his people.

"Megwetch," he said.

Then he stepped down from the podium, walked
around behind the platform stage, and went to the
bingo concession, where Goldie Kinew handed him a
cup of coffee.

"What was that all about?"

Oskinaway dropped his head, reached inside himself, and pulled out a few more words: "I don't
know, maybe I had a vision."

"Shit," Goldie said. "You wouldn't know a vision
if it were standing in front of you, glowing like a star.
You sound like the old man, dreaming of days gone,
working the mind for a spark against dead stone."

With that they both turned their attention back to
the stage, where Two Birds stood, just bending to
speak into the microphone. "I'd like to thank you all
for coming tonight, and I'd like to thank Oskinaway
for his words of wisdom tonight. I know a lot of you
won't agree with him or don't care about what he
says, but not all of you use AIM toothpaste either.
Some of you don't even brush your teeth. Some
of you don't even have teeth. Anyway, you know
Oskinaway spoke from inside with his own honesty.

"I'd also like to extend a special thanks to the senators who have graced us with their presence here. As
per their request we will have a short question-and-
answer period here, then they have to move on to
their next stop, some big rez in California, I think it's
called Los Angeles."

"Any questions? Step up to the free throw line," he
said, gesturing, with an overturned hand, to a microphone in the middle aisle of the rows of chairs.

At that point fifty people lit up cigarettes, and fifteen or twenty got up from their chairs and moved away to restrooms, hallways outside the gym, the concession stand, or to some open space against the back wall. Some people looked down at the linoleum floor, some looked up to the fans whirring in the rafters, some looked straight ahead, a few coughed, a baby cried, but no one went to the microphone.

Two Birds prodded. "Come on, these guys are here at your service."

Still no one went to the microphone.

Two Birds pleaded. "Five free pull tabs for the first four people to ask a question."

Nothing changed.

"Okay, I'll make it ten."

A young woman midway back in the gymnasium stood up and approached the microphone. She stood at the free throw line, her black boots half over the red line on the tan floor. She leaned down a bit while holding her long black hair back on one side of her face with the hand from the opposite side of her body.

"Senators," she said, "do you really want to answer the questions of these people here, or are you here because you're supposed to be here? It seems like every time someone asks a real question the answers are 'I'll have my staff check into it,' or 'According to government regulations,' or 'The best way to handle that is through your tribal representatives.' Just what do you represent?"

Two Birds reached for a microphone to temper the tone and tangle of the address to the Senator. "What I think she means—"

Senator Taylor Mack broke through Two Birds'

attempt and grabbed a hand microphone from the middle of the table where the senators sat.

"I'd like to respond to this young lady, if you don't mind, because I think I know exactly where she is coming from. As an American I too have had certain doubts about the role of our government in the administration of programmatic justice to tribes. Clearly, the history of this continent is clouded by insincere attempts to manifest human change in many people who had no desire to change. There are, no doubt, many, many bridges we must cross to understand the failures of the past and the future desires of your people so that we may all live as one in this great land. I myself have experienced high levels of discouragement in my life. As a young child I was kicked out of school for refusing to swim naked in gym class. Fortunately, I come from strong stock. My parents fought the public schools, and now no child will have to swim naked for physical education credit at any school in my hometown of Broken Lodge, Ohio. As a teenager, I was possessed by a group of powerful peers, and but for the faith of my family I would still be a man under the influence of such vile forces. As a young man going to college I was forced to take courses, for credit mind you, that presented intellectual views, in perfectly logical fashion, that run counter to the original warp and consequent weave of the philosophical blankets of our country. One professor, for example, made me research animal experimentation; another made me write a paper on my view of the corporate state. To me these experiences illustrate fundamental similarities between my life as an American of the highest moral and ethical standards and your life as a person who wishes to know what, exactly, myself and for that matter my esteemed colleagues up here on this stage have done to address important questions about American Indian policy. Believe me, you are not alone."

The young woman looked up, shook her head sadly, and said, "I'm sorry I asked. Keep the pull tabs, Two Birds."

After the senators left, a few residents of the reservation filtered out behind them like aimless gulls following a fishing boat to shore. Then, after the gymnasium doors were closed, Two Birds began again.

"I've called this meeting to bring about some kind of agreement on a problem I didn't even know existed. Look around you at this moment. Remember back to this morning, or even a few months ago, if you can remember that far back. The young people are disappearing. I don't know where they're going or what happens, but many of us are sure it's happening. It wasn't like this before, but now even our youth program counts are down."

Two Birds' gaze raced left to right and back again through the gym, occasionally resting on the hope he attached to a natural human movement, or on the interpreted depth of seriousness fathomed in a particular holding of a head, searching for a face, looking for the person who would speak up and bring some truth to a complex weave of an invisible abstract pattern of many absences that was just beginning to take form in the eyes of understanding of the community under his leadership. "Can anyone here clear this up for us?"

Finally, Rose Meskwaa Geeshik moved from a

chair beneath a backboard at the back of the gym to
the microphone standing at the opposite free throw
line. As she came forward the expression of the
crowd in the gym changed only briefly, to acknowledge the movement; then the expression reverted to
what it was before Rose moved, and at that moment
the gym population reacted as an organic whole, like
a still life come alive in thought and action, only to
turn back into a still life. On her way to the microphone Rose stepped off the center aisle momentarily
and reached out to take the hand of a young girl.
They both approached the microphone.

Two Birds took over. "Megwetch," he said. "Speak
up so everyone can hear, right into the microphone."

Meskwaa Geeshik reached out and put her lips
to the silver net at the head of the microphone. The
child stood by her unmoving, looking straight ahead,
her eyes level with the speaker's platform. Rose's
breath echoed out, preceding her words into the web
of lights and rafters at the the top of the gym. "What
I have to say isn't so important, though I do know the
story of what is happening here. I put in a request for
this meeting. Some of us have been blind to this for a
long time, you know, but who am I to go into those
kinds of things here? Many of you wouldn't believe
me anyway. Some of you might say, I remember her
when she did such and such and so and so, and that
would cast doubt for you on the truth of my words.
Others would say, she's one of those Meskwaa
Geeshiks, her father was Jake Seed, an old diviner of
some kind, her brother did this, her sister did that,
or she's trying to be smart. So I brought this little girl
up here to tell you the story. Listen to her. She may
be one of us or she may not. I found her wandering

on the road on the way back from a Big Drum ceremony out by Megis Lake. I've raised her to where
she is now. She will tell you what is happening."
   With that Rose reached down and twisted the
grooved joint midway up on the neck of the microphone stand until the microphone stood at the
proper level for the child. The child began then.
   "My brother is gone now. But before he left, he
would go out every night right when the sun was
going down. I kept wondering where he went, so I
followed him once. He went all the way to the river.
All the young people were gathered there. I watched
them all cross. Some swam, a few others took boats,
a few even had the ones who had already crossed
pull them over with a long rope, attached to a big
steel light pole on the other side. After almost all
them had crossed, I crossed over too. There's a place
over there, off the reservation. It's about as big as this
room we're in now. It has a great big sign in bright
lights, neon. The words blink off and on. I can read a
little, and the sign said The Strawberry Inn American
Café. The people went in there. The first thing you
see in the door is a big wall of smoke. Some of those
kids went into that wall and just disappeared. I got
scared and thought about going home. Then a big
Stone boy came and I stood right behind him. He
made a hole in the smoke and I went through behind
him. Inside there were lights jumping back and forth
across the room. Red, white, blue, and purple. Pipes
and medicine bundles hung from the ceiling all over
across the whole room. Pictures of Indians and skins
and old papers hung on the walls. I recognized some
of the faces, but the papers I'm not sure about. Some

of the kids carried some of those same things in their hands. They gave them to a woman behind a long table and she handed them a paper to sign. I saw people smoking all over. I saw people drinking silver, green, and gold drinks. I pretended to drink too, but I didn't. After a long time someone said you have to leave now. I don't know what happened but when those young people tried to cross the river to get back home, they couldn't make it. It was like they had turned to stone. Their arms and legs were heavy; they moved different. Many of them sank to the bottom of the river. They couldn't swim, they turned the boats over. If you go look in the bottom of that river you will see where all the young people are. They are right there among the fish and stones. I looked back into the water as daylight came and I saw them. Then I ran home."

The girl stopped, looked down, and turned from the microphone. Rose took her hand and led her back to her seat at the center of the room as Two Birds returned to a standing position at the podium onstage. Ideas swirled forth inside him, scattering churning words from an incredulous mouth like dead dried leaves outside a window of a man wondering where the summer had gone.

"Tomorrow we will go down to the river," Two Birds said. "Or we will go down to the Strawberry Inn. No, we will call government officials to investigate this matter. We'll get to the bottom of this."

Then the crowd started in, shouting suggestions from various points throughout the expanse of the gymnasium. A Weaver stood up against a woodland mural painted on yellow brick on the east side of the room. "We can't go back and get the ones who are lost or dead, but we can make a plan for the ones who are still with us."

"Aho," cried Fineday from the second row, near the speaker's stand. "We can make a plan that will prevent this problem from happening again."

Two Birds reoriented himself. "Yes, I propose we set up a committee of tribal community members to develop a plan for saving the ones who might cross over in the future."

At that point one of the two tribal planners spoke up from beneath one of the blank television screens that functioned to show close up the numbered bingo balls as they came out of the bingo air hopper, even before the bingo caller reached out to take it or see the number to call. "One option as I see it," he said, "is to build a bridge that would traverse the river and thereby diminish the danger of coming back across. Of course we would have to work out an agreement with the county about putting part of the foundation of the bridge on the other side, which is not reservation land."

At the mention of a bridge the little girl whispered into Rose Meskwaa Geeshik's ear so that when the planner was finished Rose spoke out again. "A bridge won't work. When the people come out of the Trader's place they're in such bad shape—their legs and arms are like stone—we'll lose a good many falling off."

A heated debate welled up among the people— bridge or no bridge. Committee or no committee. Soon neither end of the argument represented anything more than a dark shield with which an opponent of another's point of view could fend off poison

ideas to shoot poison ideas back. Goldie Oshawanung stood then, ready to blow up all the ideological
bridges, when old man Kinew tapped her on the
shoulder and held up his arm. With her help and the
help of a cane he rose and moved toward the middle aisle, toward the microphone. While his steps
conveyed slow excruciations of age, as he moved,
Oskinaway examined the detail of his cane. The
wood he was unsure of, but it had a reddish tinge to
it, and he knew that if someone mentioned the name
he could find the kind of tree the cane came from. At
the bottom of the cane, where the wood met floor,
the old man, or the maker of the cane, had carved
a fish; just above that an otter was shaped into the
wood, and above that, a marten. The carvings continued to the top of the cane, where the old man leaned
so much of his human weight on the center of his
palm upon the head of an eagle. Then at once, in but
a moment, he was before the people.

"A long time ago," he said, "people knew the
power of rivers, not just the power of the movement
of water, but the way the river drew life forward. So
in our learning, we learned about creeks before we
learned about bigger streams. When I was young my
great-grandfather took me to the creek at night to
learn to spear, to fish that way. He had his way, a
way that goes beyond even your remembrance. But
he took me at night. We had torches, and he told me
to walk into the water and stay still until I no longer
disturbed the water; then he said, 'Hold your torch
over the water and the light of the torch will stop a
fish right in front of you like light stops many animals. When the fish stops,' he said, 'spear it.' That
seemed simple, but when you fish this way the fish

always stops under the water in a place where the torch spreads the reflection of your own face on top of the water. So to fish this way you had to put the spear about eye high into your own reflected face. If you did that you could get a fish every time. For some reason many people can't do this; at first I couldn't do this . . . for a long time I couldn't."

At that point Two Birds nodded to two employees of the tribal senior citizens' home, who were smoking by a Coke machine near the gym doors. They rushed up and grabbed the old man. The biggest one, Gloria Morrison, gripped him fiercely by the arm, as the other, Penny Blue, said, "Enough of this, you're talking crazy again, come on old man, back to your room, the meeting must go on. Are you hungry?"

When the old man was out the door, Two Birds called on the tribal engineer, Plymouth Fury Azure, to provide possible solutions. Plymouth, so named as the result of being born in the back of a reservation car when his mother, Mary Azure, and his brothers and sisters were caught in a storm on the way back from Crane Rapids, was an enigma to most tribal members. He rarely spoke unless someone asked him to, he never socialized with the people, he didn't attend powwows, bingo, or tribal softball games. As a child people remembered him for taking engines apart, making machines out of junk in his grandmother's yard, falling out of trees as he tried to fly, and creating miniature mechanical powwow dancers. He was definitely odd, and by his senior year in high school mechanical and mathematical abilities were so apparent in him that he was offered a scholarship to Cal Polytech, MIT, and the University of Minnesota. He chose MIT. After college he returned, stranger

than ever, a bit more talkative, to head all tribal building and development projects as tribal engineer. His
childhood aptitudes and his educated genius fused
with his strange behavior and a number of tribal success stories to make him almost totally believable.

"As I see it," he began, "we have one problem, as
yet unverified, that we can hypothetically call our primary problem. In addition to that, we have a number
of other subordinate problems, which, if we manage
the primary problem correctly, can be alleviated as
well. We also have a river, which at this point has
overcome us with a ceaseless force that we have yet
to understand or utilize fully—in that sense old man
Kinew was absolutely right. As I see it, we can utilize
the force of the river to overcome attendant subordinate problems—lack of winter heat, lack of indoor
plumbing, lack of electricity—and at the same time
rid ourselves of the primary problem. That is, we can
dam the river, reroute it, pump out the part of the
river people pass over to get to the Strawberry Inn,
and at the same time we can create an additional,
tribally owned and operated source of energy, which
will serve the electrical needs of our people first.
Furthermore, we can sell the excess energy to local
communities outside the reservation to cheapen and
improve their energy resources as well. That, however, is just the horizon. Improved tribal resources
mean improved living standards; improved energy
means a more appealing investment climate for busi-
nesses who might want to venture into industrial
production on Indian land. By handling the primary
problem in the way I've suggested, we might create
infinite opportunity for growth in our community.
With the permission of you people and with the

consent of chairman Two Birds, I will begin studying the feasibility of such a project, first thing Monday morning."

Though a few reservation radicals jumped up during Azure's speculations and shouted fiery words in opposition to the philosophical, ecological, and moral consequences of such a plan, they were immediately outnumbered and outshouted by council members and tribal employees.

Two Birds' reaction reflected the reaction of most of the people at the meeting: he was astounded into a dream state of compliance. Azure's plan sounded at least like the proper course. Two Birds adjourned the meeting and almost everyone left in the earliest hours of a dark cool morning feeling good about the steps they had decided to take.

Oskinaway was tired, but he returned from the meeting the way he came, on the village road that wound around the school from the HUD projects back in the more sparsely populated sections of the community. His footfall drew the attention of dogs and sounded out the shining eyes of roadside animals. He spoke to them. He asked them who they were and where they were going; some stopped, most moved on, disappearing into deep field grass or timber stands. Dawn welled up the road then, revealing tracks unknown in darkness, thin tracks of the ones who had walked before him, tracks of wild turkeys, tracks of raccoons. He traced the track of a sparrow in a script that disappeared off the page into a ditch of dawn-struck reeds. He saw a boy there shivering, singing almost soundless in a whisper. When Oskinaway confronted him, the boy never looked up, he just kept singing. Oskinaway knew clearly the lack of cognition in the glazed surface of the deep distant eyes.

He spoke to the boy. "Hey, little brother, come out of there; you can't stay there. Hey, little brother, you must be cold; come out of there and I'll take you to my place and fix you some tea like my grandmother used to make. Come now." As he spoke he moved closer and took the child's arm, lifting him from the cold dampness of the ditch to a standing position. The boy went on singing, vocalizing an incoherence of mind and body. Oskinaway sang with the boy, and then he reached around him and embraced him, and he let the singing boy lean on him as he took him to his home. At the end of the road they turned up the two-track driveway, and he led the boy into one of the shacks where the old ones stayed. The old place smelled of dust swimming there, and the bed sang out its rust and disuse when he lay the child to sleep. Then he took off the boy's shoes, covered him, and returned to the house.

When he went into his own room to sleep, Oskinaway lay down, closed his eyes, and saw the last remnants of darkness fade from the room with the rising sun, glowing in window glare and glimmering among the shining objects that made this place his home. He reflected on the meeting, and he felt the power of the unity of community decision still living in him, when he realized that the bird hadn't greeted him the way it usually did when he came into the room. He bolted up from the bed, looked to the cage, and saw the bird at the bottom of the cage. He ran around the bed, reached into the cage, and lifted the bird. The bird breathed, yet when Oskinaway gazed into one eye he could see a light receding and coming

forward at heartbeat intervals. And the color of the
eyes changed to almost completely white. By this
Oskinaway knew that the bird had something lodged
inside it. And he remembered the veterinary training, so he squeezed the bird—in a Heimlich maneu-
ver, which is called something else on a bird—just
under the breast. Something shot out of the bird's
mouth, flashing a speck of light in the air, through
the doorway to the next room, where Oskinaway
turned just in time to see the impact and force of the
object shatter the mirror on the wall, in a brief
glimpse of his own face shattering in streaming silver
and slate black shards to the floor. Then he set the
bird back in the cage and walked through the doorway to the base of the wall, where the pieces of mirror held the room in strange confused angles. Among
the mirror fragments he found a little shell still whole
near the baseboard. He examined it, wondering
about its source, and he returned to check on the
bird.

While inspecting the bird's eye he saw that the
color hadn't completely returned to the ocular center,
and he remembered the story of how the creator
breathed through the megis shell after creating the
original man from the earth, how the creator had
breathed the breath of life into the first human, and
so Oskinaway took the shell, held it between his fingers, and placed it against the bird's beak. Then he
blew four sharp, even breaths through the shell into
the bird. He saw then a new color come into the eyes
of the bird. Blue light welled up deep in the eyes,
growing outward from the seeing center until the
light covered the whole eye, and then the eye held
there a small image of a blue dress swaying, of a

woman dancing, throwing blue light out into the room. Oskinaway set the bird down. At that moment he knew where the shell came from. He hurried through the doorway again, and he looked to the ceiling where the blue dress hung. Instead of the dress there he saw an empty hanger, barely turning in a sliver of breeze. Beneath that the blue dress lay in a heap. Oskinaway picked it up and saw that some of the shells were scattered, detached from the blue material. And he knew that the bird was healed, he knew that the bird had some power in the wing again, he knew that the bird had risen up and pulled the blue dress down and swallowed at least one of the shells. Why? He did not know—maybe, he imagined, to test its own healing. But Oskinaway decided then to let the bird go, to see if the bird could fly on its own. So he opened the door of his grandparents' house, took the bird, and set it down in front of the door.

The bird spread its wings and rose awkwardly into the air, striking the ceiling with its head. It landed where it started, spread its wings again, and lifted again. This time it flew around the room and landed just inside the doorway. Then the bird ascended again, flew around the room once, twice, three times, and on the fourth time around the bird flew through the doorway and rose into the sky. Oskinaway went to the doorway and watched the bird glide over a treeline, receding into more distant forms until it was just a thin dark vibration against white clouds. Then it was gone.

Oskinaway returned to his bed. In time he closed his eyes and he was not sure then whether he was asleep or awake, but a thin breeze blew into the room

from a crack in the open window near his bed. He
listened to the voices on the wind; the inquiry of
mourning doves dove at him from some distant wire;
the annoyance of a redwing blackbird whirled out
from nearby bushes. He heard children's voices on
the road to the school. Mission bells resonated over
them. Dogs barked out at the sound of engines. Then
the wind stopped. There was no sound, and off in
the distance he heard, "We the people, we the people, we the people, we the people." At that moment
Oskinaway rushed to the window and saw the child
he had taken in the night before slipping away into
the shadows of trees, and the source of the sound of
the words was beyond sight and then beyond sound
until he repeated the words to himself. He did that
throughout his life, often in difficult or pleasurable
situations, almost always when he was alone in the
room where the bird once spoke to him through the
limits of understanding of what the bird knew inside
and through the limits of what he saw outside in the
place that was his home.

And at times, when he remembered the words in
just the right way, when he spoke them as the bird
spoke them, he also remembered how he decided to
let the bird go. He saw the bird disappear over the
treeline at dawn from a thin vibration of black to red
underside of white cloud. Then he heard "We the
people, we the people" well up from the distance
beyond sight and he would find himself alone in
the room where his grandparents once dreamed
and talked of an old man, another Oskinaway
who came before them.